Homecoming

Heaven on Earth, Book 4

USA TODAY Bestselling Author
Reana Malori

CONTENTS

HOMECOMING
Summary

Noah Braddock

Nothing can stop me from completing the mission. Being a Navy SEAL is in my blood and I've never regretted my career choice. Until the day she walked into my life. Her voice soothed my soul. The soft touch of her hands set my skin ablaze with the need to keep her forever. When the day came that I had to leave, I had every intention to return. Then came the day I realized I couldn't. Ripping my heart from my chest, I knew it was better if I walked away. Years later, I'm back to reclaim what's mine. I've returned to the woman who owns my heart, my soul, and my happiness.

Janae Hayward

All my life I've been a good girl. Followed the lead of my parents, my church, and my community. Until the day he walked into my life. It was the first time my heart and soul were in alignment. He showed me what it meant to be fully desired. I craved him. I needed him. I loved him. Then he left without a backward glance, shattering me into a million pieces. Forced to become stronger than I'd been before he entered my world, I'm committed to moving on with my life. When he returns, it's time to decide if holding on to the pain is worth the heartache, or if I'm strong enough to grab hold of my future and never let go.

CHAPTER 1

Noah

Five Years Ago

Noah groaned as his eyes opened, the sun blazing through the curtain breaks. "Fuck. I'm tired," he muttered out loud into the empty room.

Squinting as the bright light streamed into the room, he groaned, rolling over. Sunny days still seemed to hurt the worst as his thoughts would return to the heat and desert he'd left behind. Fatigue came over him like a heavy cloak, overtaking his form as he lay on the uncomfortable mattress. These were the days he wished—maybe, but not really—that he'd become a lawyer like his dad.

Thinking about all the hours his old man worked when Noah was a kid, he put the wayward thought right out of his mind. He loved what he did. The Navy was his life's blood. He'd never made a better decision in life than when he decided to join the Navy after college.

Sitting up in the bed, he placed his bare feet on the floor. Without looking at the clock sitting on the dresser, he knew it was sometime after seven in the morning. He never slept this late. Then again, this temporary duty assignment had been rough as hell. Training seven days a week, while instructing a classroom full of Marines who felt they didn't need to listen to some guy from the Navy. Didn't seem to matter to them that the Marines were part of the US Navy. A room full of knuckleheads is what they were. They didn't think he heard them calling him Swabbie, their version of a derogatory name for Navy personnel. Bunch of Jarheads. It wasn't his fault the Marines brainwashed them into thinking they were the best military force out there. He'd like to see some of them go through BUD/s, the Navy SEAL training program, and see how they felt after that yearlong trip to Hell.

He was ready to get his ass back up to Virginia. Camp Lejeune, North Carolina was a fine installation, with a ton of history on every inch of its grounds. Filled to the brim with Jarheads and Navy personnel, it felt comfortable. Almost like home. Except it wasn't.

Planning to meet one of his buddies for breakfast, he stood from the bed. Gathering his underwear, he headed to the shower.

Thirty minutes later, he was showered, dressed, and watching the news. Of course, they weren't covering any of the shit he and his Navy and Marine brothers were doing overseas.

The secret, covert missions. Taking out dictators who cared more about money and power than taking care of their people. Changing the balance of international governments in third-world countries with two well-placed bullets. He rubbed a hand down his face as the faces of the dead played in his mind like a movie.

"This is bullshit," he mumbled before changing the channel.

Noah wasn't sure why he was so bent out of shape. He knew the work he did would never be the lead story on the six o'clock news. Not unless he had the misfortune to kill someone he wasn't supposed to. As long as he continued to kill the people Uncle Sam deemed unworthy, he was fine. Mistakes weren't allowed. Not for him and his team.

He could never lose sight of the mission due to the shit show happening in that godforsaken desert. One of his greatest fears centered around one of the civilians over there making a move he interpreted as a threat. If he killed someone who wasn't on his approved target list, he'd be all over the evening news. He was getting too old for this shit.

Maybe he needed to talk to Tyler or Daniel about what was going on his head. He'd been feeling antsy lately, like something was crawling under his skin. Tony and Ethan had reached out to tell him about the woman they'd met at Hank's gym. They were worried she was running from something. Or someone.

For some reason, they'd taken it upon themselves to watch out for her. Considering only Tony and Tyler lived in Northern Virginia full-time, he wasn't sure how they were going to do that. Ethan and Daniel were with him at Norfolk, but they all tried to make it up North when they could.

Sighing, he thought about calling his parents but changed his mind. With his dad now retired from his law firm, his parents had become young lovebirds again. Hell, they couldn't seem to keep their hands off each other. Cringing at the memory of his dad pinching his mom's butt when he was last home a few months ago, he had to hold back the imaginary bile rising in his throat. Shaking his head, he thought about what time it was back home and decided to call them later. He was sure they'd still be sleeping. And if they weren't—he shuddered at the thought. Yeah, it was best not to bother them.

His lips lifted in a small smile when he thought about the change that had come over his dad a few years ago. That's when Noah's mom had gone to the doctor for a routine check-up, resulting in a diagnosis of stage-3 breast cancer. Once the news had been given, and a second opinion obtained, Noah rushed home. Walking into his childhood home had been the hardest thing he'd ever done. He didn't know what to expect, and fear had eaten at him. Would his mother be frail and on the brink of death? Would she look like the woman who'd raised him, or had the disease ravaged her body? He'd never felt so helpless than he did at that moment.

Most of his adult life, he spent his days and nights saving the world. Yet, in this situation, his strength, shooting skills, ability to speak five languages, or his ability to run five miles in thirty minutes meant nothing. What he found when he walked into his childhood home almost unmanned him. His father, the man he'd always considered stronger than Superman©, was curled up against his mother's side with his arms wrapped around her waist. Sleeping. His mother—tiny compared to his father—was resting, while watching a television show with the sound turned low. She was still being the strong one for his dad. For him. That shit broke his heart.

She was the lynchpin holding them together. Beautiful, auburn-haired Lydia Braddock loved her family with a fierceness no one expected from a soft-spoken girl from a small town in Georgia. When he'd been a know-it-all teenager that neither the world, nor his parents understood, his mom had been the one to pull him back to the family. When his father was vying for partner at the law firm he'd worked at for years, she'd been the one to make him see his job was making him physically and mentally ill. She'd helped his father understand his desire for the next rung on the ladder was pulling him away from their family.

His dad still got the partnership, but he'd stopped working himself to the bone. No matter what, Noah's mom was the one person who could bring them back together. If she were gone, he wasn't sure his dad would survive. Hell, Noah had questions about how his own sanity would be impacted.

Noah shook his head to clear the sad memories. His mother had survived, thank goodness. Not without a lot of harrowing nights, chemotherapy, body weakness, and crying. But she was here. Thank god it was all behind them.

As soon as his mother started her battle to destroy Bob, the tumor growing inside her breast and threatening her life, his father retired from the firm. He still did a small amount of *pro bono* work and consulted with his partners on special cases. But for the most part, his parents were focused on spending every moment they could remembering why they fell in love in the first place.

It made him reevaluate his own life. Did he want what his parents had? Honestly, he wasn't sure. His career in the Navy made finding a wife, settling down, and having kids, difficult to fathom. There were times he was away for weeks without any contact with the outside world. It was hard enough worrying about getting back home safely for his own self-preservation. To bring a wife and child into the mix would make his life even more difficult. One concern he had was: would having a family make him weak? Unfocused? The next phase of his life would have to wait until the US Navy was done using him to tick the boxes on their kill-list.

Shutting off the television, he grabbed his keys and left the hotel room. Getting in his rental car, he drove over to the breakfast spot he liked. It was right outside the Camp Lejeune main gate and a short drive up the road from his hotel. Jacksonville, NC, the small city where the base was located, had everything a Marine, or Sailor, could want. Cheap restaurants. Apartments to rent. Cars to buy. Bars to drink late into the night. And, most importantly, dance clubs with beautiful women.

Arriving at the spot quickly, he swung the door open and caught the eye of his buddy sitting at a table. He'd known Heath Davis for years. They'd served together for a few years, until Heath was injured in combat. When Heath transitioned back to a full-time land job, Noah stayed in touch with him. Friends who understood his world were few and far between.

Now Heath was working at the Naval Hospital on Camp Lejeune and had the life he'd always wanted. A wife, two beautiful kids, and a dog named Duke Sparkles Goodboy. The name, Noah had been told by his friend, was the product of having two little girls, ages three and five. Although he'd laughed his ass off at the time, Noah couldn't have been happier for his friend when he'd met Stephanie and began his second life.

"What's up, man?" Heath wore a large smile on his dark brown face. Standing, they gave each other a manly half-hug before pulling back to sit down at the booth.

"Heath! Man, it's good to see your ugly ass mug. How you been? How's Stephanie and the girls?" Knowing the menu like the back of his hand, Noah didn't have to look at it to decide what he wanted. Although, he knew one thing he did want. *Coffee.* Catching the attention of the waitress, he called her over.

"My ladies are good. Driving me up the wall, but I'm okay with that. With Kayla turning six this year, Stephanie went back to work."

The waitress stepped up to their table, grabbing their attention. "What can I get you gentleman this morning?" she asked, pouring black coffee into both their coffee mugs.

Noah and Heath both gave their order. The waitress gave them a smile, departing from their table without writing anything down. Didn't matter though. This place didn't have a fancy menu, and neither he nor Heath were complicated. Meat. Potatoes. Eggs. Toast. Coffee. The breakfast of champions.

Looking over at his friend, he noticed he still had a big ass grin on his face. "Ah, shit. I know that look."

Not even attempting to hide that he was up to something, Heath kept on smiling. "Stephanie wants to see you. Said it's been too long. The woman thinks you're avoiding her."

Hanging his head, he tried not to grimace but couldn't stop his face from scrunching up in disgust. Looking back at his friend, he grunted, leaning back as he stirred cream in his coffee.

"Do you remember what she did the last time I was here? Because I sure as hell remember," he spat.

He wasn't really upset with Stephanie. Matter of fact, he loved the woman like she was his sister. In many ways, she was.

She'd accepted his friend without question. Hadn't cared one bit about his wounds, scars, or that he could no longer save the world while only armed with a 9mm pistol, M-16 rifle, and a special issue K-bar knife. Stephanie had taken one look at his friend and fell head over heels in love. Now Heath saved lives in a hospital instead of taking them. Giving people back their life with the use of a scalpel and a damn steady hand.

"Oh, yeah. I remember. Wasn't that the time she set you up with that chick Julie?" Heath was holding back a laugh as he spoke.

If Noah could get away with punching him in the face without Stephanie getting upset with him, he would. *Asshole*. He knew exactly what happened.

"Man, fuck you. That woman was horrible. Her laugh. Her voice. I swear, she was talking about family vacations and planning my departure from the Navy." He'd run from her as fast as he could. Noah had been disappointed in himself for spending any time with her at all.

No longer able to hold it in, Heath's laughter rang out in the small restaurant. Several heads turned their way.

"After you left, she called the house at least two times a day. Constantly asking Stephanie when you were coming back down or if you'd mentioned her. Man, she was crazy as fuck. I told Stephanie not to do that shit again. That you could find your own dates. She didn't like it. She wants you happy, or so she says. Personally, I think she's trying to torture you."

Blowing out a deep breath, he nodded, "Well, that shit's working. God, I love that woman, but she should be in PsyOps. Are you sure she's a legal secretary? Did you have her checked out?" At Heath's raised eyebrow, Noah raised his hands in surrender. "I'm just saying. That woman is a force to be reckoned with."

"That she is." Just then, their waitress came back with their food. The men were silent as they spent a few minutes shoveling food in their mouths. After a few moments of lips smacking and large gulps, Heath spoke up. "Oh, she's out today with one of her friends from that law firm she works at. Getting waxed and buffed, or something like that. She was gonna stop by and say hi if we were still here when they came through."

"That's cool. It'll be good to see her. Where are the girls?"

"With her parents. Some church event for the kids. I swear, I've never seen people go to church as much as they do down here."

"Well, this is North Carolina. What did you expect?" Noah questioned with a smile on his face. The people down here were quite serious about their religion. Not that he didn't believe in God, because he did. He and the Big Guy had plenty of talks when he was doing the will of his country. But he'd also become cynical enough from the evil things he'd seen done to other human beings to have bucketful of doubts about God.

To his way of thinking, religion seemed to be a method of holding people back from questioning right and wrong. He didn't begrudge those who used their faith to get through the hard times. Great for them. But for him, doubts filled his mind. Questions he couldn't stop asking continued clawing at him. From his experience, he'd seen people use religion as a crutch when they couldn't explain the world around them. Something people held on to when there was nothing else.

"I know. I know. But damn, it just gets to be a bit much. Stephanie's parents aren't so bad, but the hypocrisy of good vs. evil is in full effect. As my grandmother used to say, 'All church folk, ain't good folk'."

Nodding his head, Noah agreed. "You got that right, Brother."

The ding over the restaurant door sounded, just as Heath's face lit up. "There she is now. Hey baby," he called out, standing to greet his wife.

Placing his napkin on the table, Noah stood to give Stephanie a hug as well. Grabbing her up, he held her tight, twirling her around. "Hey, Stephanie. You ready to leave this zero and get with a hero?" It was their standing joke.

"You're so dang crazy!" She laughed when he released her. Punching him in the arm, she fussed at him. "Why haven't you been down here to see us? The girls miss Uncle Noah."

"Ouch, woman! Quit assaulting me," he howled in fake anger. "As long as you stop beating me up, I'll be over before I leave."

Rolling her eyes, she turned her head to look at someone behind him. Her lips lifted in a smile, and her eyes got a wicked gleam. "Hey, Janae."

Noah turned around to greet her friend. The sight before him stole his breath. Her hair was long, straight, and styled in a high ponytail. His gaze floated over her face, her skin the color of his favorite soft caramel candy. Hazel eyes framed by thick, long lashes. Lips so lush, he wanted to lean in and kiss her. He didn't give one shit that he didn't even know her full name or anything else about her. Including, if she already had a man. His stomach felt funny, which had never happened before. Unable to turn his gaze away from her face, it took a moment before he noticed her hand was outstretched to him.

"Hi, Noah. I'm Janae. It's so nice to finally meet you in person. Stephanie's told me so much about you."

Fuck. Even her damn voice was beautiful.

After a nudge in the arm from Stephanie, he looked over at his friend's meddling wife. Her eyes were wide as she kept motioning to her friend. "Aren't you going to say something, Noah?"

Turning back to Janae, he extended his hand, grabbing her smaller one in his larger appendage. "Nice to meet you, too. Goddamn, you're fucking beautiful."

CHAPTER 2

Janae

Five Years Ago

Janae noticed the two large men standing with Stephanie when she came around the corner. She'd stopped at the restroom when they'd first arrived. Too much coffee and water when she'd woken up this morning. The "too handsome for his own good" black man facing her was Stephanie's husband. She hadn't met him before, but, based on the numerous pictures strategically placed around Stephanie's desk, and the stories she'd been told, she felt like she knew him already.

From the way he looked at his wife, she could tell he truly loved her. Smile faltering a bit, she felt a pang of envy slice through her body. One day, she would have a love like theirs with a man who looked at her as if she hung the moon in the sky. A God-fearing man who understood church was important to her. Well, better yet, important to her family. Therefore, it had to be important for her as well. Her parents would never forgive her if her husband wasn't right with the Lord.

At twenty-seven, she shouldn't care what her parents thought. However, their wants and needs for their children had been ingrained in her from the time she could form words. Didn't matter that she didn't want the kind of life they led. Her parents didn't have a bad life, because from what she could see, they didn't. Where she differed from them is that she didn't see herself living in Jacksonville, North Carolina until she died of old age. Bored. Unfulfilled. Stifled. A lifetime full of regrets. This was not the life she wanted, but it was looking more like this was the life she was going to get. And honestly, it fucking *sucked*.

Sighing, she forced her smile to remain in place as she approached the trio. The other man standing next to Stephanie was larger than Heath. His arms were visible since he wore a short-sleeve T-shirt and blue jeans. Black boots covered his feet. Giggling to herself, she wondered where his leather jacket and motorcycle were. Short, dark hair covered his head, but his broad back begged for a longer look. Damn, the man was built.

She wasn't an innocent by any stretch of the word, but this man made her want to sin. Sin again. Then sin a little more. She'd never dated a white man. Hell, she'd never seen any of her friends' date outside of their race. Definitely not while growing up. Even now, as adults, none of the women she'd grown up with dated anyone other than black men. A sudden visual of large pale hands trailing up her darker skin raced through her mind. *Stop, Janae. Your mind is getting ahead of you.*

Her words would have had more impact if he'd never turned around.

If only she'd never seen his ruggedly handsome face. If only his chest hadn't looked to be carved out of granite. And those gorgeous pink lips. They looked soft, juicy, kissable. Just the way she liked. And why did his eyes travel up and down her body, as if she were a gift delivered from the heavens just for him?

And then he spoke.

"Nice to meet you, too. Goddamn, you're fucking beautiful."

Her body quivered in response. Nipples pebbling at the gravelly tone. Shocked at first, she could only look up at him with a smile on her face. Standing five feet six inches on her best day, this guy Noah had to be at least six feet two. Maybe even six-three. Either way, he looked like he could pick her up and throw her over his shoulder, before making off with her to his secret lair.

And now she was getting fanciful. Yup, this Noah character had blown her mind within thirty-seconds of their meeting. She was in so much trouble.

*****

Six Months Later

"Everything about you makes me want you even more," Noah's gravelly voice filled her ears as they lay in bed.

"You know we can't lie in bed all day."

Giggling, she snuggled closer to him. His broad chest served as her pillow. His long limbs were wrapped around her much smaller form like a blanket. His body heat warming her from the chill lingering in her bedroom.

Since that first day, he'd been the only man on her mind and in her dreams. His name was the one on her lips as she pleasured herself in the darkness, remembering their times together. The thought of their lovemaking had her body squirming. The things he could do with just his tongue, one finger, and those succulent ass lips had her quivering.

Whoever said white men didn't know how to throw down in the bedroom clearly had never met Noah Braddock. If she had anything to say about it, they never would. Feelings she never thought would happen, bubbled over as she nestled within his strong embrace. They'd seen each other every chance they could. Either she went to him in Norfolk, or he came down to North Carolina. She knew he had a dangerous job, but they never talked about it.

Ever.

For her, it was a matter of don't ask, don't tell. If she could avoid the reality of knowing Noah was out there risking his life, she could live in oblivion. For him, she was positive his job had a clearance level preventing him from saying much, if anything. She wasn't stupid though. Living around a military base her entire life, she knew how things went down.

She'd seen so much over the years living in this area. Guys who came back with post-traumatic stress. Those who ranted and raved about the people they'd killed. The friends who'd been killed, or worse, lost limbs in front of them. They'd talk of the ongoing damage to the countries they visited, the despair of not knowing if they would live or die. The unending desire to end the pain they were feeling.

Tears would flow down their faces as they questioned why the US military was over there in a foreign country in the first place. How they could send men barely into adulthood to a country that didn't want them there. They didn't understand why their country chose to protect people who hated everything it stood for. And all the while, she saw resentment and disdain grow inside many service-members who just wanted to live their lives in peace, serving their country without giving up their lives.

No. She didn't want to know the specifics about what he did. As his woman, her role was to comfort him. Hold him when he needed it most, even when he tried to deny it was what he wanted. Her job was to give her man peace. When they were together, there was nothing else to interfere with their time.

Rubbing her hand on his chest, she kissed the tattoos covering his skin. "Why do you have so many tattoos?" When he failed to answer her, she looked up, expecting to find him dozing off. He wasn't. Gaze bright, he stared down at her with a look of hesitation on his face.

"Do you really want to know?"

Looking in his face, she knew the answer wasn't going to be something she wanted, nor expected. This wasn't a story of how he got drunk in college and decided tattoos were his life. Turning her focus back to the large expanse of skin, she bit her bottom lip, her hand hovering a little closer. This time, instead of mindlessly grazing over the skin with the soft pads of her fingers, she took her time. Eyes wide open, her fingers slowly traced the tattoo patterns covering the bare skin of his chest.

Without saying another word, she allowed her soft touch along his skin to tell her what she couldn't bear to let him voice out loud. Ever so slowly, as she moved her fingertips along his skin, she felt ridges. Small sections of puckered skin.

Tears fell, the wetness trailing down her face. Her breath stuttered in her chest.

"Janae," his soft, gravelly voice called out to her.

Shaking her head, she forced the words out. "No. Let me do this. We don't talk about what you do. I know this isn't a topic we usually allow to get in the middle of our time together. On any other day, I'm okay with that. But this time, I asked the question." She paused to take a deep breath before continuing. "If I can't understand that you risk your life for me, for this country, and it could possibly someday lead to you getting hurt, or worse, then I don't deserve you. Please, Noah. Just let me do this."

"Baby," his voice was thick, filled with something she couldn't describe.

Taking a deep breath, she lifted her gaze to his. "You are so beautiful. You know that, right?" To her, no other man in the world could take his place. Everything about him was rugged and handsome. The shape of his jaw. His crooked smile. The roughness of his hands gripping her tight. Her man had scars and puckered skin from years of battle.

Noah was a warrior through and through. And he was all hers.

His lips lifted at the corners. "Men aren't beautiful. But you… well, you're a damned siren sent to bring me to my knees. Forcing me to worship at your feet."

Tingles traveled through her body at his words. She loved this man so much. At that thought, she froze. Could she feel so strongly about him so soon? Yes, she could. She did. She wanted him with every fiber of her being. They'd make it work. Even if it took months or years of interstate travel. They'd find a way. They had to. Right?

Looking at the clock, they had another three hours before they'd be forced to get dressed. They were meeting Heath and Stephanie at their house for lunch. They were the only ones who knew about her and Noah. That was how they both wanted it. For now, anyway. Pretty soon, things would need to change.

She wasn't looking forward to the confrontation or the relentless questions from her parents. But she'd been playing house with Noah for far too long now. If they continued in secret, it would be viewed by her family and friends as embarrassment.

Some may even view it as shame of Noah and their relationship. Neither of those assumptions were true, but facts would no longer matter. Perception would rule the day. Granted, she'd hesitated with him. Taken their relationship slower than normal but it was only because she was being cautious. Janae wanted to make sure this thing between them was authentic before causing chaos and upheaval within her family. They'd both need to be willing and able to weather the storm if they had any chance of making it to the other side.

Noah moved his thick, muscled body closer to hers, nestling between the warmth of her legs. Pressing the limb against her nether lips, he moaned. "Are you tender?"

Deciding to throw him off his game, she shifted to the side, pushing him onto his back. Rising over him, she adjusted her form, straddling his hips, her bare pussy resting on his thickening length. "Not at all. As a matter of fact," she leaned down, kissing his neck. Tracing her tongue along the sensitive skin under his ear, she moved her lower body. "I want more. Are you gonna give me what I need?"

"Baby, I'd give you the fucking world if I could."

"All I want is your cock inside me," she whispered in his ear. His hands jerked to her waist. She felt his manhood become thicker as his mushroomed head pressed into her tight passage. Using one hand to reach back and grab his length, she positioned her warm opening over his cock before pressing the tip against her. "Always so good," she couldn't help but mutter. "Fill me, Noah." Releasing him, she allowed gravity and their combined need for each other to do the rest.

"Look at me," he growled.

Opening her eyes, she caught his gaze. What she saw reflected caused her heart to skip a beat. There was no denying this was real. Noah slid deep inside her as they stared at each other, and they both moaned once he was fully seated. "Noah," she whimpered.

"Janae."

"I—I..." she wanted to say the words but knew this wasn't the time. You never say those three words in the heat of sex. They lose their power. She'd just tell him later.

"It's okay, baby. I know. I feel it too." Grabbing her by the neck, he brought her face down to his. Kissing her softly, he released her lips before laying her head in the crook of his neck. His other hand rested on her lower back, pressing her firmly down onto his as he lifted his hips.

Their lovemaking was slow, soft, perfect. Noah was everything she'd hoped for and dreamed of for so long. Wrapping her arms under his shoulders, she held on while he took her where they both needed to go. Wetness fell from her eyes as she basked in the love of a good man. A protector. A warrior. He was hers, and she was his. Finally.

*****

Six Months Later

Janae walked up to her parents' front door. She knew this day would come. Looking over her shoulder, she wanted to get back in her car and drive back to her house. Today wasn't the day for this. They had church tomorrow. Her father hadn't been feeling well. No. Today wasn't the day to have this conversation. Just as she turned around, intent on returning home, the door opened.

"Janae? Baby, why are you just standing out here on the doorstep without coming in?"

Her mother's sweet voice beckoned her. She wanted to turn around, but her body wouldn't move. Tears began to flow down her cheeks. It wasn't supposed to be like this. Noah was supposed to be here with her. Standing by her side. Proclaiming his love of Janae to her parents. Both putting on brave faces as they thumbed their noses at old prejudices and bigotry.

Instead, she stood alone. Angry. Hurt. Confused. He'd been gone for six months, with no call nor an email. Not even a message sent through Heath or Stephanie. Nothing. Maybe it was her almost declaration that she felt something more for him than just sexual attraction. Maybe it was the need for him shining in her eyes whenever he held her close, their bodies entwined in passion. Or so she thought.

"Janae," her mother called out. Her tone sharper in the ensuing silence.

Taking a deep breath, she turned around. Might as well rip off the bandage. Speak the truth and shame the devil.

"Hi, Mom. I'm sorry it took me so long to stop by. I've been having a hard time lately."

Her mother's eyes bulged. The older took a step back. Her hand rising to her throat, she stared at Janae's stomach. "Janae? Baby? You're pregnant."

"Yes, I am." She tried forcing her lips into a smile but could sense the moment she'd failed.

Her mother looked down at her left hand. Then looked around, as if searching for someone. "Come inside. Are you alone, or are we waiting for someone else?"

Shaking her head, Janae balled her fists. "No. No one else, Momma. It's just me." Stepping inside her parents' home, she'd never felt so alone or betrayed.

She was carrying the child of a man she loved and hated with equal fervor.

A man who'd abandoned her without a word.

Heartbreak and embarrassment were constant companions.

The constant stares and murmurs from friends and strangers alike had become too much. She was surprised no one had gotten to her parents before she did.

Alone and pregnant by a man who'd promised her the world, shown her what life could be, enticed her with seductive words and amazing sex, while looking at her as if she were the only woman in the world.

In the end, all he gave her were broken promises.

She had no idea what she was going to do.

CHAPTER 3
Noah

Four Years Later

Noah didn't know why he was here. This was a bad idea. Too much time had passed. Would he be welcome? If he tried to explain, would she even listen?

Sitting in his truck across from the small house in Jacksonville, he questioned for the tenth time if he was doing the right thing. So much had happened during the time he'd been away, he wasn't sure she was even the same person. Was he?

What he'd felt for Janae had been real. There'd been no other woman he'd wanted more than her. No woman who made him long for more than what he had. Hell, he hadn't even wanted the whole family dream. Not until her.

Then he'd left her alone.

Running his large hand down his face, he rubbed along the short beard growing there. Typically, he liked to be clean-shaven, but with his job, he couldn't always have it the way he wanted.

Kids riding their bikes passed in front of the truck. Their loud, exuberant yells as they called out to their friends or laughed, made his lips twitch and lift in a grimace. Had he ever been that young? That carefree? He felt as though he'd always been the guy he was today. Grumpy. Jaded. Cynical. And, according to his adopted sister Adele, much too serious because he didn't seem to relax or smile very often.

Noah didn't have time for any of that. Nah, that kind of thing was for young fools and people who deserved a life of carefree happiness. That kind of thing was for people who hadn't lived in hell for weeks or months on end and seen the worst in people on too many occasions to count.

Maybe he was being too cynical. He could relax; hell, he even smiled when around his friends and family in Virginia. Ethan, Daniel, Tyler, Tony, Adele. Even that fucker Stefano, his sister Adele's husband.

Those were the people who understood him. They didn't need him to express shit he didn't feel like discussing. The world he'd lived in for all these years was not for the weak, nor those with a conscience. And all in the name of honor, country, commitment. For his country. The Navy. His SEAL team. Even still, he couldn't escape the regret filling him. His dreams—nightmares—were filled with the nameless faces of the people he'd killed, and their families who wept over their lifeless bodies.

In the daylight hours, he could hide behind the façade of just doing his job and following orders. They all did. Those who couldn't handle it, either got out on their own or were helped to leave by Command. That's not something he was concerned about. He'd lost his conscience a long time ago, as the body count continued to rise. Unfortunately, for the government-approved enemy, he was damn good at what the Navy needed from him.

He wouldn't admit it to many, but he loved the thrill of what he did. To be honest, that feeling worried the fuck outta him. Closing his eyes, he thought about his last mission. It had shown him his perspective was changing. In the past, he'd give himself a speech about what he had to do and why he was doing it. Reminding himself about the importance of the mission. He'd repeat a silent mantra about the national security of his country, and how the democracy of the country his team was helping was at risk. It had been what he needed. That was then.

Not this last time. As Noah had waited for his target, he felt nothing. No remorse. No questions about the morality of what he was doing. No need to remind himself why he was there, in that place, ready to take the lives of people he'd never met, spoken to, or even seen prior to this mission. The sound of his breath was the only thing he could hear, his eyes were steady and focused on his target. His finger on the trigger.

Just the slightest movement, invisible to the naked eye, changed so many lives. The almost imperceptible whizz of the bullet as it left his rifle. Even as the hole appeared in his target's head, he still felt nothing. He remembered his thoughts clearly from that day, *"One down. Two to go. Let's dance, motherfuckers."*

Sighing deeply, he glanced at the kids as they rode to the end of the street, only to turn around and begin riding in the opposite direction.

"Never lose that innocence, kids. Because once that shit's gone, you'll never get it back," he muttered into the quiet space of his truck cab. And now, here he was, acting like a fucking stalker, sitting outside the house of the only woman who'd made him feel human. The one who was there before the darkness began to take over.

Adele, his self-adopted sister, was able to penetrate the hard shell that had grown over his heart. But the love he had for her was different. With Adele, he was still in protector mode and probably always would be. From the first moment he and his not-so-merry band of friends had brought her into their world, each of them had known there was a reason she'd shown up in their lives. There was somewhere, or someone, she was running from.

Each of them swore an oath to protect her at all costs. Never again would she need to feel afraid, or alone, or that she had no one to turn to. She was their sister. It didn't matter if her blood didn't match any of theirs. She was theirs by choice. No one would get the chance to hurt again. Not on their watch. Heads would roll, and blood would spill before any motherfucker came for their sister. Rubbing his hand along his chest near the black, twisted organ some would call a heart, he took a few breaths to try and calm down. When she'd finally admitted to them what happened to her, in North Carolina of all places, he'd seen red.

The only thought running through his mind was how long it would take him to find her ex-husband. Could he make the trip to North Carolina and back within a day? Did he have enough Sodium Hydroxide to dispose of the body?

Since he didn't at the time, he'd been ready to ask Daniel to borrow some of his secret stash. Daniel would have given it to him too, but not before inviting himself to join "Mission Kill that Son of a Bitch" first.

Laughing as he thought of his friend, he shook his head at the image Daniel portrayed to those who didn't know him. The persona of boy scout fit him well, until all hell broke loose. Daniel was a man not to be trifled with. He may seem like the sweet one. Quiet. Shy. Low key. That façade had fooled many people over the years. That dude was a straight-up killer. A shiver went down his spine as he recalled some of the "hypothetical situations" he'd shared with some of the guys. Daniel was one guy he'd never want to meet in a dark alley on a bad night. Some shit just wasn't worth it.

Noah looked down at his watch, noting the time. He'd been out here waiting for over two hours. He knew his intel was correct, but he needed to see it for himself. When he'd gotten the call from Heath, he knew his life was going to change forever. Closing eyes, he thought back to the day his whole world imploded.

He was late getting to Adele's house for their regularly scheduled cookout. Without a doubt, she was going to fuss at him for arriving after the expected start time. Being late wasn't his thing, but there was no getting around it, he'd had a shitty night of sleep. He hadn't been to his Northern Virginia home in over two months. Thank goodness he had a cleaning service come in every two weeks, even when he was away for long periods of time. In Norfolk he rented a small apartment to serve his needs when he needed to be close to base, but this was his home.

Three bedrooms, two-and-a-half bathrooms. A large kitchen with marble counters with a separate island in the middle that held the flat stovetop. He'd had the basement remodeled into his perfect man-cave, including a sixty-foot television for the football games. Yeah, this was the place he usually felt most comfortable. But not last night. He was antsy, fidgety, nervous. As if he were about to go on an unknown mission with spotty intel. Only thing is, he wasn't. Shaking his head, he began walking to the door when his cell phone rang. Looking at the screen, he saw Heath's code name displayed, Black Panther.

With a smile, he answered, "'Sup, man?"

Heath's sigh came through the phone, making Noah pause. "Ghost, we gotta talk." That Heath was calling him by the name only a few men knew, told him this call wasn't just for shits and giggles.

"Damn, man. You alright?" When no sound came through, Noah backed up into the house. Shutting the front door, he sat down in one of the living room chairs. "Okay, it's just me. Talk."

"You need to get back down here to Jacksonville." Heath's voice sounded tired but firm.

"You okay, man? Stephanie? The girls? Whatever you need, just tell me. When do you need me?" He knew the questions were coming fast and furious, not really giving his friend a chance to answer. The tone of his voice said something was seriously fucking wrong, and Noah didn't like this shit one bit.

"Slow down, Ghost. Damn," he paused. *"I can't believe this is some shit I have to tell you over the phone."*

Taking a deep, calming breath, he growled, *"Tell me what the fuck is going on, Heath."*

"It's Janae."

As soon as Heath said her name, Noah's heart stopped. Visions of the last time he saw her filled his mind. He'd left early to head back to Virginia. Still sleeping soundly in her bed, Noah leaned over to kiss her before heading out to leave. Turning back, he'd looked at her with longing and the uneasy feeling he wouldn't see her again. His gaze took in every inch of her body, as if memorizing her face, her form, and the memory of her lying in bed, the sheet covering only half her body. His dick thickened with the need to take her again, but he'd held back.

How was he to know it would be the last time he'd see her? It was now just over four years later, but it seemed like yesterday when he'd left her. That Heath's call was connected to Janae made his palms sweat. He almost laughed at the irony. He never let any situation take him out of his comfort zone, but just hearing her name had him bouncing one leg as he rubbed his sweaty palm down one side of his jeans. Finally finding his voice, he finally spoke, "What about her?"

"You just need to get down here. When you asked for my help with Janae a few years ago, we respected your wishes. We didn't tell Janae what you'd gone through or why you weren't calling. Man, I was in the doghouse for months over that shit."

Noah knew all this. Didn't need Heath to rehash it. When he'd told them he couldn't see her anymore, he'd only asked that they support him, no questions asked. Noah later admitted to Heath that thoughts of Janae had fucked with his head. Thinking about her screwed with his focus on missions. Missing her had him all messed up and distracted. He had the bullet wound to prove his words were true after he'd been shot on what was to be a simple extraction. There'd been no question about what had to be done at the time.

All ties to Janae had to be severed. There was no other choice.

But now, here they were again. Her name was like a cold glass of water on a hot summer day. After he'd made the decision to cut ties with Janae, he'd shut down the piece of his heart tattooed with her visions of her smile, her kisses, the words of love she never said, but he'd seen in her eyes every moment he was in her presence. As if waking up from a long slumber, the shadowed, dark place inside him where the memory of her lived began to hum with life, and that shit hurt.

"Heath," he heard the strain in his voice. Knew Heath would have picked up on it as well. "What about Janae?"

"We hadn't seen her in a few years. At least, I hadn't. Stephanie had. And... man... Janae has a kid. A daughter." Heath paused, as if waiting for Noah to respond.

What was he going to say? She'd moved on. He shouldn't be jealous, but he was. Even though he knew it wasn't fair to expect her to live her life waiting for him to return, he was still angry another man had lain with her. Fucked her. Made a baby with her. That should have been him, but he'd been too damn scared to take the risk.

"Why are you telling me this? Really, Heath? Man, I didn't need to know this shit," he was practically yelling at this point.

"If you'd shut the fuck up, I'd tell you why I'm calling. Janae's little girl is four years old."

Noah's heartbeat stuttered to a standstill before slowly beating again. The sound of the thumps rushed into his ears as he felt the organ beat against his ribcage. Four years old. Which meant... No. It couldn't be.

"She's four?" His voice was barely above a whisper.

Sighing in the phone, Heath continued. "Yeah, she is. I'm sorry, Ghost. You should have been told. Stephanie's in the room crying and feeling sorry for herself because I told her this shit was foul. You should have been told as soon as she found out about the baby. If Janae was hurt about what happened or didn't know the best way to tell you after you'd broken things off, Stephanie should have told me. She knew part of the reason you walked away. Stephanie's known you since the first day I met her. You were the best man at our wedding. Her loyalty should have been to you."

Noah was seething. How could Stephanie keep this from him, or from her own damn husband? She knew the fucking deal but kept this from him as if it were a fucking game.

"Heath, just to make sure I'm hearing you right. Are you telling me Janae had my baby? That I have a little girl? Are you sure?" He waited anxiously for his friend to answer.

"Yeah, I'm sure. Her name is Nicole."

"Nicole," he repeated.

"She seems to be a perfect mix of you and Janae. I saw a picture of her. She looks like you. Not to say you shouldn't get a paternity test. Just... Fuck. Yeah, she looks just like you, only prettier." Another pause, which Noah was thankful for. "Noah, you need to get down here to Jacksonville."

Coming back to the present, he saw a champagne-colored vehicle pull into the driveway. Watching the scene play out in front of him, he held his breath as he waited for Janae to exit the car. He wanted to be angry with her for what she'd done, keeping his child away from him. Noah also knew he was partially to blame for the situation. Watching Janae from the inside of his truck across the street, the feelings bubbling up to the surface had nothing to do with anger.

Desire. Need. Want.

After all this time, it still felt like she was his. That she belonged to him. He knew that was a stupid thought, but it didn't matter. Nor did it matter that he'd hooked up with the occasional Frog Hog, women who were always around, seeking out a man who'd give them a night to remember. All they wanted was the bragging rights to say they'd bagged a SEAL for a night. And one night was all they'd get from him. He had no use for anything longer than that. They both knew the deal. When they'd both gotten what they needed, each went their separate ways.

That was his past and had only been a way to pass the time. None of that mattered now. What was most important, was the gorgeous, tawny skinned woman opening the back door of the car. Reaching in, she helped a little girl climb out. As the little girl reached the ground, she began waving her hand at the kids riding by on their bikes, and they waved back at her. "Nicole," he whispered. As soon as Noah saw the little girl's smiling face, he knew she was his. Even from this distance, he could see the dimples in her cheeks. The same ones reflected at him in the mirror, even though he didn't smile enough to show them often.

Dark, curly hair cascaded over Nicole's small shoulders. With skin the color of light beige, she was clearly mixed with black and white. Beautiful. She was absolutely fucking beautiful. And she was his. Well, half his, but still. He had a little girl.

How was he going to make this right?

CHAPTER 4
Noah

Lifting one hand to his face, Noah was surprised to see he was shaking. Fear? Nerves? Anger? All the above?

She'd had his child. A little girl who looked so much like him, it made his heart hurt. His daughter was being raised without him, her father. How could she do this to him? She should have told him. Turning his gaze back to Janae and Nicole as they walked into the small house, his eyes turned hard with anger. Was he being irrational considering he was the one who'd left her without a word?

Yes, but it didn't matter.

She'd carried a human life inside her body. One he'd helped her create. His daughter was born into this world without his knowledge. A picture of Janae swollen with pregnancy entered his mind, and his breath caught. He'd missed it all. Every moment of her growing from a tiny pea to a

Homecoming

full-size human baby. Noah had been robbed of so much. Even the privilege of being in the room when she was born, had been snatched from him. Fuck this. She wasn't going to hide his daughter from him any longer.

Grabbing his phone, he dialed Heath's number.

"Hey man," his friend greeted once he picked up.

"What the fuck, Heath? Why wouldn't she tell me?"

A long sigh came over the phone, "Ghost, listen to me. According to Stephanie, that woman has been through hell. When you left, she lost it. Wouldn't get out of bed. She stopped eating. When she began throwing up in the morning, Stephanie forced her to go see a doctor. They both thought it was due to not eating or just feeling down. That's when they found out she was pregnant."

"Are you telling me your wife knew this entire fucking time? Why wouldn't she tell me? Tell you?"

"Hell, I don't know man. She's been in tears since I found out. She, uh, wants to see you."

"No."

"Come on, Noah. You can't avoid her forever."

"I can sure as fuck avoid her right now. Her loyalty was to me," Noah yelled into enclosed cab of his truck. "She's known me since the two of you began dating. I considered her a sister. She married into the family. That alone means something to me. I thought it meant something to her also."

"I hear you. I do. Just...fuck. Hear me out. Apparently, once Nicole was born, Janae was put through some shit."

"What do you mean she was put through some shit?" Sitting up straighter, he felt his body tense as he waited for Heath's next words.

"You remember this is North Carolina, right? This state hasn't quite moved on from the 1950s. It's not hard to see Nicole has a white father. And Janae isn't married. Apparently, there are quite a few people who like to share their opinions about her situation."

Anger rushed through Noah at what Heath was saying. There was no fucking way this was happening. Glancing at the closed door of the home protecting his woman and child, his fists tightened. That anyone would say something negative about them, or to them, made him want to put a hole through the steering wheel.

Then again, he had only himself to blame. He should have been there. Never should have left Janae on her own to begin with. He didn't know she was pregnant, but it didn't matter. He knew what she felt for him, what he felt for her in return. Pushing her away at the time was best. He'd needed to focus on the job. She'd become too much of a distraction when he was in the field.

At least that's the story he told himself.

"Are you telling me she's been getting shit ass comments said to her because she had my child?"

"Yeah, that's exactly what I'm telling you. From what I know, she's lost friends she's known since childhood. Her parents' church turned their back on her."

"Fuck," Noah couldn't help yelling.

"Yeah. I know you're angry about this situation. So am I. Wait, hold on." Noah heard Stephanie talking in the background. "Not right now, Steph. Just let it go for a bit…When he's ready."

Noah could only imagine what she was saying. He loved her, but right now, he had no words for her. Not sure if he ever would again. Looking down at the clock, it was a few minutes after two o'clock. Heath's voice caught his attention.

"Hey, sorry about that. Stephanie wants me to tell you she's sorry."

Noah ignored the apology. "I need to talk to Janae. She needs to explain to me why she kept this a secret from me all these years."

"Shit, you know I hate getting in the middle of women's shit and their feelings. Makes me uncomfortable as fuck. You know that, right?"

"What's your point?" His patience was waning. He wanted to see his daughter's face up close. Allow her to see him. He wondered if she'd recognize herself when she looked in his face. Would she know she was a part of him?

"She thought you were ashamed of her."

"What?" Noah couldn't believe what he was hearing. "Where the fuck did she get that idea?"

"You just fucking left, Noah. No word. No nothing. You forbade us to say anything to her about you. You swore us to secrecy.

Had us tell her we had no idea where you were or how to reach you. We used your job as a cover. It was the only thing I thought could work. Apparently, she didn't buy one fucking word."

"Damn," he whispered. Noah knew he'd fucked up. He knew it the moment he'd walked away from her that morning. "I was never ashamed of her."

"I know that. Then again, I'm not the one who had to go begging to my parents with a baby growing in my belly with no ring on my finger."

"I didn't know—" he began.

"Doesn't matter. That's what happened. I called you because you needed to know. If I'd known what was happening, I never would have condoned that shit. You're my brother. What they did was foul no matter how they try to spin it. But here we are. So, now that you know, what are you going to do about it?"

They talked for a few more minutes before hanging up. Noah clenched his hands tight, deploying some of those relaxation methods he'd been taught. Blood rushed through his body at such a furious pace, he could hear the sound in his ears.

He had a daughter.

He had a daughter. With Janae.

He had a daughter. With Janae. The love of his life.

The woman he'd abandoned because he was afraid of what being with her would do to him. Make him weak? Or maybe he'd lose focus on a mission and be shot to hell and back. Then what would have happened? He would've been half the man he was today. Too many of his buddies had been left high and dry after coming home with missing limbs and shattered souls. He didn't want to give her a chance to rip his heart out because she wasn't tough enough to handle the bad along with the good.

Taking a few deep breaths, he prepared his mind for the greatest challenge he'd ever encountered.

Get out.

Walk up to her front door.

Let her know he was back.

Tell her he knew about Nicole.

Pray like hell she didn't slam the door in his face.

Fighting with her in the past had been fun. Mainly because each fight usually ended with out of this world make-up sex. In the kitchen. In the shower. On the floor. Leaning over the dining table. His thick rod hardened at the thought of how her body felt when he sank inside. The memory of their bodies twisted together, writhing in passion as they expressed their feelings for each other in actions, if not words, never failed to make him pause.

If he were honest with himself, he missed her. Her voice. That sweet laugh she had. The deep sigh as she snuggled close to his body after he'd fucked her every which way he could. Leaving her behind had been the hardest thing he'd ever done. It felt like he'd ripped a piece of his heart out, leaving it on the dry desert floor to wither and die.

"Get your ass moving, Noah," he lectured himself. Grabbing the door handle in his tight grip, he exited the truck. Closing the door, he looked around the neighborhood. A few people were walking along the street, some biking, and others sitting on their front porch. It wasn't a bad location at all. The homes looked well-kept, with front yards full of fresh green grass covered with children's toys. Just the kind of place a small family would want to live.

The thought pulled him up short. Had Janae moved on with another man? Gotten married? Maybe she was seeing someone.

Did it matter? *Not one bit.*

Would it stop him from seeing his daughter? *Hell no.*

On the other hand, if she hadn't moved on with another man, what did that mean for the two of them? What if just the thought of being with someone else turned her stomach? No other woman had compared to her. He'd tried to be with other women, to push the memory of their time together out of his mind. The first time he tried, his dick wasn't having any of it. Had sat there limp no matter what the pretty blonde had done to him. Hell, he'd even gone to the bathroom and given his dick a stern talking to, eventually pleading with the lump of flesh to cooperate.

That night, and many others, he slept alone. Whenever his dick got in the mood to rebel against being inside anyone other than Janae, Noah would be left with blue balls as he dreamed about the woman he'd left behind.

Laughing at the embarrassing memories, he continued walking across the street. He should have known he'd never get over Janae. Those other women were just fill-ins who left him unsatisfied and with one less condom.

Janae was in his blood. Her scent still floated around in his brain. The remembered taste of the sweet nectar of her pussy made his mouth water. Even now, just being near her, knowing they would be face-to-face, his cock was thickening in his jeans as he thought of the two of them in bed.

"Traitor," he mumbled.

Noah walked to the house. Committed to seeing this through but scared shitless of a little person no taller than his knees, he wiped his hands along his pants. This was one of those moments he needed to talk to his father. How the fuck was he going to be a good dad to Nicole when he couldn't even be a good man to her mother? His job had him traveling all over the globe, doing shit for his country that should make him ashamed. Only it didn't anymore. He was proud of who he was and what he did for the US Navy and would never apologize for it.

Didn't that say more about him than anything else? If he could take a man's life without blinking an eye, or feeling one bit of remorse, was there something wrong with him? He didn't want his child to be someone like him. Someone who only cared for those closest around him. A man who routinely shut off his emotions to let the darkness seep into his soul.

He didn't want that for Nicole. He wanted her to grow up to be like her mother. Sweet. Caring. Loving. A woman any man could love. Too bad he'd seen her first. Any man who thought he was safe from Noah ever returning was shit out of luck.

So, no, it didn't matter if there was someone else in her life. If she wasn't married, he'd remove all barriers standing in the way of him being with her again.

Arriving at the front door, he heard squeals of laughter. Knocking on the door, he waited expectantly as he heard the locks disengage. A few more minutes passed after it seemed the locks were undone. He knew what he would find on the other side.

Janae must have checked the peephole. Looked to see who was outside before allowing them access to her home and her child. That she'd paused, not opening the barrier standing between them, told him what he needed to know.

"Open up, Janae," his loud voice called out.

"No," he heard her respond.

He almost smiled but didn't. God, he loved this woman. After all these years, his feelings for her hadn't diminished one bit. Just hearing her voice did something to him. Now that he was back in town, there would be nothing to stop them again. He'd make sure of it.

"Let me in, Janae." He tried to make his voice sound soft and non-threatening. "I don't want to scare her the first time we meet, but I'll kick this motherfucker down if you don't let me in." There went that battle. His nerves where shot and his temper was short. He knew his threat was irrational. Kicking her front door down would be the easiest and fastest way to have the cops haul his ass off to jail, ensuring his chances of being part of his daughter's life would disappear.

Silence on the other side was the only thing he heard. Leaning his head against the thick wood, he gave a silent prayer to the man upstairs. He couldn't walk away. He wouldn't. No moment in his life was as important as this one right now.

"Don't leave me out here begging. She's my daughter, Janae," he pleaded. Noah was a card-carrying bastard of the worst kind. He didn't deny it. And anyone who knew him could attest to it. But now that he'd found out about Nicole, everything would have to change. He'd be a better man if only to make his daughter proud of him. *Please*, he begged silently as he waited for Janae to decide. He just needed Janae to give him a chance. A final lock clicked, and Janae's face came into view as the door swung open. Once his eyes landed on her, he exhaled.

"Hi, Noah," she greeted him with a soft tone.

"Damn. You're still so fucking beautiful." His blurted words were reminiscent of what he'd said to her the first day they'd met.

Only, this time, she didn't smile in response.

"Come in." Stepping aside, she gave him room to enter the home. As he stood in her living room, they could only stare at each other. With everything he knew, he knew his face held looks of anger, confusion, and surprisingly, need. As he watched her stand in front of him, he licked his lips in remembrance of their time together.

Hips a tad wider. Breasts bigger. Thighs still thick and curvy as fuck. Her straight hair was pulled up in a ponytail on top of her head. After four years, she looked almost exactly as he remembered. Even better actually. There was a maturity about her that beckoned him. He wanted to grab her up, rip her clothes off, and shove his dick into the best fucking pussy in the world.

"Baby," he murmured as he took a step closer.

Her head shook from side-to-side, refusing him. He was about to grab her, lift her in his arms, when a voice called out.

"Mommy? What are you doing? Who is that man?"

CHAPTER 5

Janae

Eyes bugging out her head, Janae stared at Noah as he stepped over the threshold to her home. When she'd first seen him standing outside, her heart had dropped to her stomach. That he'd showed up on her doorstep wasn't surprising. She'd known this moment would happen eventually. Either he'd come searching for her on his own, or Stephanie would break her silence.

From the look on his face, she was positive Stephanie had squealed like a pig. She loved that woman like a sister, but she was a damn snitch, she thought with a huff. No, that wasn't fair to Stephanie. Janae knew asking Stephanie to keep a secret this huge was pushing it. In all honesty, she was surprised the woman held out for so long. Every time they spoke or went out for a bite to eat, her friend was constantly asking her if she could let Heath know. And Janae always answered the same. "I'd rather you didn't. Just give me more time."

Unfair as hell, but she hadn't cared. Not until this exact moment. Closing the door, she sighed in defeat.

Noah still looked as good as she remembered. His broad shoulders. Dark brown hair. His beard was short and trimmed up nicely, which she'd always loved. Then again, when he had his full-beard going strong, the sensation on her inner thighs when he went down on her was soul-quivering good. Taking in his larger than life form as she stood in her too-small living room, she bit her bottom lip nervously.

When her daughter interrupted the moment, she broke her gaze from him, walking over to the little girl. "Hey, Punkin'. This is mommy's friend from a long time ago. How about you draw your grandpa a picture? Okay?"

"Okay, Mommy." Nicole gave Noah another long stare. It was the look of someone trying to figure out something that was just out of reach. With how smart her little girl was, Janae wasn't surprised at anything she did. To be so young, Nicole was performing tasks usually completed by kids aged six or seven.

Getting her daughter settled, she turned back to Noah. His gaze was planted firmly on the four-year-old girl with the long curly pigtails. Nicole tilted her head to the side as she concentrated on the man in front of her. Interestingly, Noah did the same thing. That's when Janae saw it.

Of course, she'd always known Nicole was Noah's daughter. Plus, she looked like him, the only difference being her darker skin and her feminine features. Janae looked on in awe as she watched the two of them in the same room for the first time. Tears welled in her eyes as she noticed one of her daughter's behaviors reflected in the man she'd loved more than her own life. No, her love for him hadn't ended. She'd pushed it back to the recesses of her brain, and heart, because of his betrayal. Looking at him now, Janae knew her love for him was just as strong as it had ever been.

The beautiful little girl sitting at a kid-size table with crayons and markers, was the only person she focused on now. All the love she'd had in her heart for Noah was given to their daughter. For Janae, from the moment she was born, Nicole was the only person who mattered. Needing to take the conversation away from little person ears, which seemed to always hear the things parents didn't want them to, she moved toward the kitchen.

Noah lifted one eyebrow. "Going somewhere?"

"Moving our conversation into the kitchen. Maybe this isn't the best thing for her to overhear."

After a long pause, he turned back to Nicole, as if he couldn't take his eyes from her. His legs began moving before he focused back on Janae. "Fine. Lead the way."

Once they arrived in the kitchen, they stood mere feet away from each other. For so long, Janae had thought she was ready for this conversation. She wasn't. Hell, she'd planned every word she'd say to him if their paths crossed again. In that moment, her mind blanked.

Hands shaking, her nerves almost took over. Yes, she was in the wrong. Then again, so was he. Giving birth to their daughter, and not telling him about it, wasn't something she did without thinking through the consequences.

Noah just stood there. Not saying a word. His eyes flashed with anger as he stared at her. His lips were thinned, pressed together, and one eyebrow raised in question. His legs were spread wide, his arms crossed over his large chest. Those emerald green eyes of his glared at her with a hard glint.

She could see the confusion practically swirling around in his heated gaze. Truth be known, she didn't want to have this discussion with him right now. The longer they stood there, the more heated she became. She was the one who should be pissed at the situation. Not him. "Why are you here, Noah?" Might as well go on the offensive. After all, he was the one who'd left her.

"No, sweetheart. You don't get to do that. I think I'm the one who needs some information. Don't you think? When was she born?"

Crossing her own arms over her chest, she turned away from him. Screw him. He was the one who left her without a word. She'd been on her own to face the crucible while he'd been off gallivanting, probably screwing women all over the globe. Damn.

She'd been such a fool. To be honest, she still was. "Does it matter when she was born? Why do you care anyway?"

"Don't play with me. Not right now. Do you know how it felt for me? To find out you'd had my child? My d-d-daughter."

She heard the stutter in his words. The raw emotion almost made her weaken and give in. Janae was three seconds away from begging his forgiveness. The hurt in his tone generated this need within her to plead with him to forgive her. To tell him she never wanted her or Nicole to be a burden. Back then, she thought she was doing the right thing. Being noble and all that shit. The only thing she'd done was made herself an outcast, someone who lived a half-life because she'd loved the wrong person.

She remembered walking up to her parents' house with a belly full of baby. A child put there by a man who couldn't be bothered to tell her himself that he no longer wanted her. Scoffing at him, she glared at his large form. "Are you for real right now? Your daughter, huh? Weren't you the one who promised you'd return? You're the guy who told me what we had was special, right? You know, the man who claimed what we had was real? Yet, when you disappeared without a word, leaving me no way to reach you, what was I supposed to do?"

"You could have found me," he almost yelled.

"Fuck you, Noah," she hissed. "You don't get to walk in my house, where I live, and try to tell me what I should have done."

"Don't ever speak to me that way again," he growled. Walking towards her, his face was a mask of rage and anger. "I had every right to know about my child!"

"Not when you left here like a bat outta hell. My daughter and I have been doing just fine, thank you very much. Where were you when I was walking around here with your child growing in my belly, embarrassment on my face, with humiliation running through my veins? Off playing the hero, when all you are is another man who wanted to get his dick wet. When the going got tough, your sorry ass left town and never looked back."

A smirk came over his face, "I wasn't the only one getting wet, sweetheart. If I recall, you enjoyed what we did as much I did. Don't blame me because you got a surprise at the end."

Anger coursed through her veins. Lifting her right hand, she swung towards his face. Her intent was clear. Remove the smirk from his face by any means necessary.

Noah caught her hand in his, holding it inches from his face. The smirk remained, but his eyes blazed fury. "I wouldn't do that if I were you."

Snatching her arm away from him, she bared her teeth. A female lion ready to pounce. "Don't you ever touch me again." Stepping away from him, she cursed as tears began to well in her eyes. "Why are you here? You left me, Noah. Not once did you look back to see what you'd left behind. You didn't want me back then. Why show up now?"

"Things have changed. You have my daughter. Now that I know about her, I'm not going anywhere."

The clipped tone of his voice had her on edge. He wanted a fight, probably deserved one, but he was about to be disappointed. Taking several deep breaths, Janae tried to calm down. He had no idea what he was asking of her. Had no clue what she'd gone through or the questions she'd been asked about the father of her child. He was oblivious to the looks and whispers happening behind her back for years. Now he waltzed back in her life as if he had every right to be there.

He didn't!

She'd been heartbroken when he'd left. Her soul had been torn into pieces. There were times she'd wanted to roll up in a ball and die. Yes, it had been that serious. For the first time in her life, she had thought she'd found real love and acceptance. A man who'd be her protector. Someone who would choose her above all others. Only he didn't. She'd been played for a fool. Something like that was hard to get over.

Her body did all the things it was supposed to, but she'd been a shell of her former self. Food held little appeal for her. She'd lost more weight than was healthy. Since she couldn't get out of bed for two weeks, she'd called in to her job, requesting some time off. Hell, even Heath had come to check on her to see if there was anything medically wrong with her. It had been a cursory check, done at Stephanie's request. But still, he'd come to her home to make sure she was okay.

Yet, here Noah stood. The man who'd sent her down a spiral of despair and heartache. He had the nerve to press her with questions, demanding answers she didn't want to give. Nor was she prepared to do so. Her life was finally getting to a good point. She no longer cried herself to sleep at night. People had gotten used to her and Nicole. They no longer pointed and whispered as she sat in church on Sundays. Hell, she'd even started dating again. There wasn't anyone serious, and none of them had been introduced to her daughter, but she was starting to explore options. And in one moment, he'd snatched away all the progress she'd made. Hurled her back to the days when darkness and grief were her constant companions. He must have gotten tired of waiting for her to speak, because his next words were meant to cut her deep.

"I'll take you to court, Janae. I'll fight you for Nicole if I need to. You won't keep me away from my daughter." Noah paced in front her, his hands stuffed in the pockets of his jeans.

Shocked at his words, her arms dropped by her side. "You'll do what?"

"You heard me," he snarled.

Who was this man? She'd been such a fool to believe his lies. "Noah, you haven't been around her since the day she was born. You had no idea she existed until recently. Which again, if you'd allowed your friends to tell me where you were, this could have been resolved, long ago. Or if you'd sent me a message—just one—to let me know you were okay. To explain. I tried so many times to reach out to you. Yet, you ignored me. I know how this works."

Shock filled his eyes. Janae knew it wasn't because she was wrong. It was because she knew what he'd done. "What do you mean?"

"Stop the lies. I know you were hiding from me. You forget Noah, I knew Stephanie before I met you. She'd tell me how Heath had a group of friends, you included, and no matter where they were in the world, they could get to the other person. Based on what you do in the Navy, I know you wouldn't always be free and accessible. But let's not insult my intelligence. If Heath needed to find you, he could get a message to you. You knew I was looking for you. You just chose not to respond."

He ran a large hand over his short hair, stepping back from her. "It was for the best."

Closing her eyes, she begged the tears not to fall. "Why, Noah? I spent months wondering where you were. Questioning why you hadn't called. Asking myself if I'd done something wrong."

Shaking his head, his gaze became intense. "It had nothing do with you, Janae. But trust me, it just had to be done. I thought I was ready for something more. I wasn't. Leaving you was probably the best thing for both of us."

"No, Noah. It wasn't." Looking over his shoulder at her daughter, she shook her head. "Your actions caused you to miss out on one of the most precious gifts in the world. You don't even know her."

Turning his body so he could look at their daughter, she saw the look on his face soften. "I had no idea. If I'd known, I would have returned. Come back here to Jacksonville. Been here for you as much as I could. I'd never leave a child of mine on their own, without a father. That's not who I am."

Janae watched him closely. Something inside her began to melt. During the time they'd dated, she'd gotten to know the softer side of Noah through his stories of family, friends, along with some of their antics.

Maybe that's why it hurt so much when she realized what was happening. That he was done with her. Had thrown her to the side like yesterday's garbage.

"I want time with my daughter. Are you willing to give me that? I have the next week off from duty. I want to spend time getting to know her. Don't deny me. Not this."

Everything inside her wanted to say no to his request. To turn him away without a second thought, the same way he did her. Thinking about how this would change things for her child, Janae prayed she was doing the right thing. She was worried about her own sanity as well. Nicole was too young to go off by herself, especially with a man she didn't know. Janae didn't believe Noah knew anything about taking care of a rambunctious little girl. Which meant, not only would Nicole be around him, but so would Janae.

She'd just have to make sure she protected her heart. The last thing she needed was to allow her love for Noah to take over, only for him to show his true colors. That was the last thing she wanted, especially since she'd tried to convince herself, and her parents, that she no longer loved the father of her child. She knew it was a bald-faced lie, but to convince her parents, she first had to believe it herself.

"She doesn't know you, Noah. I'm not going to leave my child with a strange man."

Offended, his upper body jerked in response. "I'm not. I'm her father."

"She doesn't know that. To her, you are a man she doesn't know. One who doesn't look like her Papaw. You will give her time to get used to you. And until she does, I will be with you every minute." Shaking her head, she wanted to laugh at the entire situation. Then she wanted to cry. How did she get in this mess?

"I would never hurt her," he whispered. "You don't trust me around her?"

She could tell he was hurt by her words, but she didn't care at the moment. Her daughter was the most important person in her world. There was no way she'd put Nicole in an uncomfortable situation. If that was his expectation, he could leave right now. Shrugging her shoulders, she looked up at him. "Those are the rules. Take 'em or leave 'em, but that's what they are. You choose."

After a few moments, he took a deep breath before answering. "Fine. I'll accept your terms."

Looking at the clock, she noticed the time. "If you want to stay for dinner, you can. It'll just be fried chicken and garlic mashed potatoes."

Nodding, he looked relieved. "Yes, I'd like that."

Returning the motion, she took a deep inhale. "Okay, let's go talk with our daughter. Follow my lead." She noticed Noah rubbing his hands over his hair again. His nervous tell. "Listen, before we do this, you need to be sure. Once we start down this road, you can't decide it's too hard. There's no changing your mind or pulling away. You must be one-hundred percent committed to this. No matter how tough things get."

"What makes you think I'm not?"

"Just be sure, Noah." She was nervous as hell about this whole thing too. Nicole had started to ask where her daddy was since she was noticing her friends with both parents. Janae knew that's why her daughter had been staring at Noah with wide eyes when he walked in the house. None of the men in their lives looked like Noah, so by default, he was a curiosity.

"I'm sure. I'm not going anywhere."

Janae remembered a time, five years ago, when he'd said the same thing to her. She could only hope he didn't break their daughter's heart the way he'd crushed hers.

"Fine. Let's go meet your daughter."

CHAPTER 6
Noah

Noah felt calmer today. Yesterday, when he'd first shown up at Janae's house, he'd been full of hurt, anger, confusion, combined with a whole lot of fear. That was the one emotion he could do without. It made grown men do stupid things. Like leave the woman you loved without so much as a goodbye or explanation.

Fuck! Rubbing a hand down his face, he thought about this entire fucked up situation and knew he was in trouble. Like "the real deal-fucked up-he'd be making this shit up for the rest of his life," kind of trouble.

Get him in a gun battle in the middle of a warzone and he was on his 'A' game. Send him on a mission to rescue a high-value asset from the middle of B.F.E (Butt Fuck Egypt), and he was all for it. *Hoo-Yah*!

But this right here? Introducing himself to a little person who stood no taller than his gun belt? This shit made him want to run for the fucking hills and call-in for backup and an extraction.

He knew, without bias, of course, that she was the most beautiful little human he'd laid eyes on. Once he'd seen the perfect form of his daughter's face yesterday, he knew he loved her. Even though she didn't know who he was, his little girl had stolen his heart, and he was happy to hand it over. The need to protect her came over him in a wave. This little person, who could barely tie her shoes, was rapidly turning him into a big ass softie. Knocking on the door to Janae's home, he held a small brown teddy bear in his large hand. Corny? Probably. He was new to this whole *father*-thing, so felt he could take a mulligan or two.

When the door opened, Janae stood in front of him looking gorgeous, as usual. Wearing a pair of tan Capri bottoms, white sandals, and a blue shirt, she looked like an everyday suburban mom. He couldn't help but think about what was under those clothes, however. The soft curves that cradled his large body when they used to make love, the spot under her ear that made her squirm with need, the feel of her nails as they scored his back the deeper he fucked her. He wanted to press her against the wall and take her lips in a sensual kiss. She may think he no longer loved her, no longer wanted her, but that was the furthest thing from the truth. He'd never stopped wanting her. It was his own stupidity that made him walk away from her. Now that he was back, he'd make damn sure he never left her again. He didn't care how long it took to convince her.

Last night, he'd been on his best behavior. Plus, he'd been blinded by the knowledge of his daughter. If he looked at it from her perspective, he knew she had every right to think he wouldn't be interested in a child. The way he left... yeah, that had been a bitch move. He could call it out for what it was. After their conversation in the kitchen, which wasn't as secret as they thought it was, they'd entered the living room to find Nicole staring at them.

Her gaze bored into him with laser focus. Even as Janae explained to her that he was her daddy, Nicole never looked away. Her eyes tracked him from his feet to the top of his head. Leaning back against her mother's chest, the small child didn't give him one inch.

Smiling a little at the thought, he could admit he felt pride swell in his chest. She wasn't going to let just anyone come in here and get close to her or her momma. Yup, she was definitely his child. Even if she had blue skin and purple eyes, he'd know it. Her mannerisms, her distrust, her curiosity. All of it was identical to him. His mother had shared enough stories about his childhood and his "precocious behavior" as she called it, for him to recognize the signs.

Oh shit!

He had to tell his parents. His mom was going to give him shit for years about this. This hole he'd dug just kept getting bigger and bigger. *Fuck!*

Janae's voice broke into his musings. "Hey, Noah. Are you sure you want to do this?"

His woman... *Janae,* was twitching and shifting from side to side. Her fingers tapped along the side of her thigh. He remembered her doing this whenever she was concerned about something. It would be odd that he recalled her tendency to do this if he hadn't replayed every moment of their time together. Every word. Every kiss. Every moan he pulled from her body. Plus, there hadn't been another woman of importance in his life since he'd left her. That's not to say he didn't take care of his needs. He did. Hell, half the time he was just trying to get the picture of Janae riding his cock out of his brain. Shit never worked anyway.

"Why are you nervous?" he asked, stepping into the house.

"What? I'm not." She tittered.

Yeah, she was nervous as fuck about something. "Are you gonna tell me what's going on in your head?" If he needed to press, he would. Just then, Nicole bounded into the room. A smile came over his face as he noticed her pink tutu.

Today was a ballet recital at her dance class. Noah had never seen any type of dance or event with ten tiny humans, but he was sure it would be fine. Right?

"Hi, Sweetheart," he greeted Nicole as she came to him with her shoes in hand. Ah, the dreaded laces. During their getting to know each other session last night, he'd found out shoelaces were not her friend, bedtime was for babies, and she wanted a dog named Princess.

Her eyes kept going to the teddy bear, who just happened to be wearing a pink tutu, like the one his daughter was wearing.

"I got this for you today. Maybe you can hold her while we go to your dance school."

Glancing up at him with an intense look in her eyes, she grabbed the bear, then handed him her shoes. "Okay. Shoes, please."

Picking her up in his arms, he walked them over to the couch. Sitting them both down, Noah attempted to put on her shoes while she babbled away. As he struggled with this task, Nicole ignored him while having a full-blown conversation with her new toy.

"Bear."

Lifting his head, he was prepared to face a nine-foot grizzly barreling into the house. Since no sound of a door being ripped apart, or the roar of a killer animal could be heard, he turned to Nicole. "What, sweetheart?" Maybe he heard her wrong.

The miniature version of the woman he loved, looked at him with a large smile covering her cherub face. "Her name. Bear."

"I think she's telling you she named the bear, Bear." Janae came from the kitchen area with a full backpack.

"What's that for?"

"Change of clothes, just in case. Snacks. Just stuff we might need while we're out and about." Glancing around as if she forgot something, she suddenly took off towards the back of the house. "Ballet shoes," she called out to explain.

Noah looked down at Nicole and noticed her watching him. Shrugging his shoulders, he smiled at the little girl, "I think Bear is a great name." Finishing up her shoes, he patted her legs, "Okay, all done." Although it seemed like such a small thing, the fact that he was doing this task for his own child shifted something inside his chest.

"Okay, let's go. If we don't get on the road, she'll be late. I'm always late for these things. I think I'm single-handedly keeping the stereotypes about black women alive and well."

Giving her an odd look as they walked out of the house, he questioned what she meant. "What's that supposed to mean?" Pressing the fob to unlock his truck, he led them to his large vehicle.

"Hmmm?" Looking in the direction he was leading them, she shook her head. "Nothing. Don't worry about it. I'm just rambling. Oh, we can't go in your truck. We need a booster seat for her."

Smiling, he knew this would come up. "I grabbed one last night when I left. Installed it this morning." He knew it was done right too. He spent an hour pouring over the instructions and reading all the safety information included in the packaging. Hell, he'd even stopped by the local fire station to have the guys do a double-check. Just the thought of Nicole not being safe or injured in any way made him break out in a cold sweat. As long as he was alive, he'd make damn sure his daughter was protected. If he could build a bubble around her, he would.

"Okay, let's go get in the car." Noah watched his family walk out of the house in front of him. Something hit him in the chest, heart squeezed tight, and his breath came out in ragged hiccups. Noah didn't understand what was going on or what he was feeling. Being away from them so long, he'd missed so much. Looking in the eyes of his daughter, he realized he'd made a terrible mistake. Walking away from Janae had been the wrong decision. Keeping her in the dark for so long had been the wrong decision. He never should have left.

"Hey, Noah? Are you coming?" Janae asked as she stood still in the front door of the house.

Shaking his head, Noah gave her a small smile, "Yeah, I'm coming." He needed to clear his head. He needed to make sure Nicole didn't think he was uncomfortable with her. Just looking at Nicole as she walked towards the truck with her mother, he knew this was where he wanted to be. With the woman he'd fallen in love with so many years ago. With her and Nicole, the little girl created from their love. Protecting them both. He didn't know what he would have to give up for them. To have them by his side. But he was willing to do just about anything.

"All right, up in the truck," he called out, walking up to his vehicle. He was hesitant to pick her up without permission. In her eyes, he was a large, gruff, unknown man. All this was new to her. She didn't really know who he was or his place in her life. Nicole didn't know he'd give his life protecting her. To this perfect, but tiny person, he was a stranger.

And that part hurt him the most. If he had known about her, he never would have left. If he could go back in time, have one last redo, he never would've left in the first place.

"Noah, it's okay if you pick her up. She may need some help getting into your truck because it's so large." Janae smiled at him softly, noticing the way he fidgeted. Covering her mouth with her hand, he knew she didn't want him to be embarrassed. It didn't matter to him anyway, maintaining his cool points wasn't his focus. Janae knew what he was going through, and if she took a bit of pleasure in his discomfort, so be it. He was positive she'd gone through the same thing, and since she'd made it to the other side, so would he. The uncertainty of what to do when a little person could twist you in knots. His emotions were reflected on his face. But fear overpowered everything else. He wanted to do the right thing. Needed to show Nicole her dad was a good guy. That even though Noah hadn't been here for the first years of her life, he was here now. For that reason alone, he appreciated Janae's attempt to give him an opening to build a connection with Nicole.

"Nicole? Is that okay?" Suddenly his palms were sweaty, as if he were unsure about what she would say. His nerves were getting the best of him and he stood to his full height, ready to accept the rejection he knew was coming.

Nicole nodded her head as she lifted her arms up towards him. Taking the opportunity in front of him, he knelt to pick up his child. Holding her in his arms, he felt his eyes fill with water. He didn't know it would feel so good to have her little body next to his. This little human he'd helped create would change his world for the better.

From now on, someone would always call him daddy. She'd look up to him with innocence and the unwavering knowledge that he'd always fix things. She'd always love him, no matter what. Even with all his flaws. The feeling was unbelievable. Hell, he needed to call his parents.

His eyes misted and his vision became blurred when he thought about all he had missed. He swore to himself, right then and there, he'd always be there for Nicole and

Janae. Nothing would prevent him from being there for them in the future.

Opening the door to his truck, he glanced over at Janae and gave her a small smile. Mouthing the words 'Thank you,' in her direction, he watched as she nodded in return. Her own eyes glistening with tears as she took in the sight of him holding their little girl.

CHAPTER 7
Noah

Once they were all loaded in the truck and buckled, they made their way to Nicole's dance studio. Although it was only twenty minutes away from Janae's home, it seemed to take forever to get there. With how slow he was driving, he was surprised it didn't take over an hour. Laughing to himself, he realized he'd been petrified driving with Nicole in the back seat.

His hands were white-knuckled on the steering wheel as he drove down the road with lanes that were too close together. Sweat broke out on his brow as he'd worried about every vehicle on the road. So much, it was practically dripping down his face. Once they arrived at the ballet studio, he turned off the truck, sat back in his seat, and blew out a long breath. The silence in the truck was deafening. Janae and Nicole could probably hear his heart beating out of his chest.

He'd growled at every car that came within inches of his vehicle. Didn't they know he had precious cargo on board? During the long ride over, he'd also decided it was time to get a new vehicle. The one he had was no longer good enough. Not enough safety features. It was a flimsy tin can just waiting to be crushed. If that happened, he'd have to call on the brothers to come raze the entire fucking city of Jacksonville. Didn't matter that others might say he was overreacting. Clearly, those people didn't know he had a *daughter*. Because if they did, they'd keep their damn mouths shut.

All he could think about during the entire drive were the other drivers losing their shit for a minute and plowing into his truck, hurting his daughter. How the hell did parents function every day? He needed to make some phone calls. Nicole needed a driver skilled in defensive driving techniques. Janae needed to get trained also, and Noah needed to buy her a new car. The one she had wasn't good enough for her and Nicole. Not anymore. Stefano probably knew people who could put some additional steel reinforcements in the doors and replace the windows with bulletproof glass.

"Noah? You okay?"

Noah jumped at the sound of Janae's voice. "Damn! You've been sitting here this whole time?" He smiled at her, trying to downplay his reaction. Of course, he knew she'd been there but he'd gotten lost in his own thoughts. Ignoring both her and the little girl looking at him strangely from the backseat. He almost lifted his hand to check for horns growing from his hairline.

Janae burst out laughing. "Really, Noah?" She kept a smile on her face as she looked at him with a quirked brow. "Seriously," she motioned to him still gripping the steering wheel as if their lives depended on it. "Are you okay?"

"Yeah. I'm fine." Saying the words didn't change the pace of his breathing. His heart was beating rapidly, almost as if the adrenaline wasn't slowing down.

"You don't look fine."

Taking a deep breath, he glanced at her. "Is this how it feels every time?"

"What do you mean?" He noticed her smile had gotten wider.

Yeah, he felt like his eyes were opened to the world around him for the first time. This feeling was completely foreign to him.

"It's not funny, Janae. Does it always feel like this when she's in the car? That sense that everyone else is crazy and none of them deserve to have a license or drive on the open road? That they're going to do something stupid, and your child will be hurt?"

Janae shook her head. Not to disagree with him, but to say she understood. "For the first year of her life, it felt exactly like that. I was scared to go outside of the house. I was afraid to drive down the road. All I could think about was protecting her. I was a crazy lioness protecting my cub."

Noah rubbed his hand over the place where his heart lay, the thump of the organ in tune with her every word.

"In the winter, I had her bundled up in five layers of clothes." Pausing as she laughed a little under her breath, she looked at him with a soft smile. "It does get better. It just takes time. Once you get used to her being around, you won't get the heart-pounding fear every time you go out in public."

"Mommy, are we going into class now?" Nicole's voice called out from the back seat of the truck. They both jumped, laughing as they realize they'd gotten lost in their own conversation.

"Yes, baby, let's go." Janae got out of the car and went around back to open the door to let her little girl out.

Noah took a few more deep breaths. "Life will never be the same again."

With all the things he'd learned over these past two days, he needed to make some changes for the future. Getting out of the truck himself, he walked around the front to meet Nicole and Janae. He was excited to see his little girl in her dance class, to watch her show off her talent; but was less than thrilled his first outing with them was to ballet. Not that he wasn't comfortable in a ballet class around a bunch of three- and four-year-old little girls in pink tutu's, but it wasn't his normal scene. Maybe he could convince Janae to sign her up for peewee soccer or t-ball. He wondered if girls could play peewee football. Now that was an idea he could get behind. Since Tyler still coached the team up North for five-and six-year-old boys, he'd have to check with him on that.

Speaking of Virginia, Noah smiled at the thought of telling the guys about Nicole. If they could see him now, they'd laugh their asses off. Then again, maybe not. His brothers were more than just boneheaded muscle men. They cared about each other. Once they found out about Janae and Nicole, he was positive they would bring them into the family and love them as much as he did. The only issue was that he still needed to tell the guys about his ready-made family. They'd have questions he wasn't sure he was prepared to answer.

Walking inside the ballet studio, Noah could tell something was wrong with Janae. She was fidgeting and twitching again, her eyes shifting around the room looking at the women sitting in tiny chairs in the too-bright space. As soon as Nicole ran over to the changing area to take off her coat and change out of her shoes, all heads turned in the direction of the door looking for the person who'd brought her.

A small group of women stood off to the side staring at Janae. The looks on their faces weren't necessarily hostile, but neither were they welcoming. Their eyes looked her up and down, smirks on their lips, and not one of them spoke. Noah was off to the side, walking around the room getting a feel for how everything was set up. And although he wasn't standing directly next to Janae, he didn't miss anything happening around her. Her eyes were downcast, and she hurried over to an empty spot where there were a lot of chairs but no people. As soon as she sat down, Janae lifted her chin, straightened her back, and pasted a smile on her face.

Her deliberate behaviors raised questions in Noah's mind. What the hell was that all about? Walking over to her, he sat down in one of the empty chairs next to her. His long legs were splayed out in front of him as he leaned back in the too-small seat. These chairs were not made for men like him. Hell, they weren't made for men at all. Just as he went to ask Janae what was going on with the other women, Nicole ran over with her ballet shoes in her hand.

"Mommy! Mommy! Can you help me with my shoes?"

"Of course," Janae responded with a huge smile on her face. Lifting their daughter onto the chair next to her, she quickly slipped her pink ballet slippers onto her tiny feet and tied the straps. Janae gave their daughter a hug, kissed her on the cheek, and told her good luck. Nicole went running off to join her friends when she stopped, turning around to look at Noah.

His heart stuttered in his chest. He didn't want to ask for acknowledgment or a hug, but he desperately wanted one. He knew he was asking for too much. She'd only just met him. But even after spending such little time with her, he felt like he'd known her all her life.

Nicole walked slowly back to Janae and Noah, her eyes never leaving his face. As soon as she was within a foot or two of them, she turned to her mother. "Can I give daddy a hug, too?"

Shocked at her words, Noah looked over at Janae who was nodding her head, "Yes, baby, you sure can."

Nicole walked slowly up to Noah, lifting her arms to wrap them around his neck. Grabbing her closely, he gave her a hug that he hoped conveyed to her how happy he was that she'd accepted him, even if a little bit. "You're going to be the best ballerina out there." He knew his voice was wobbly through the words, so he cleared his throat to try and get his bearings. He didn't want to sit here with tears in his eyes and choked up with emotions during her entire practice.

Damn it all if he didn't want to just bask in the feeling of hearing her call him daddy for the first time. He wanted to take his daughter, and his woman, away from this place. Just wrap them in his arms and protect them from the world around them. He wanted to get to know Janae again so they could get back to where they were all those years ago. Noah wanted to understand what she'd gone through while he'd been away. He wanted to know what those looks were for from the other ladies sitting on the other side of the room. Because he didn't like this shit one bit.

As soon as Nicole walked away, he turned to Janae. "Thank you for letting me be here today."

"I would never keep you away from Nicole."

Noah raised his eyebrow at her statement. Hadn't she done just that? Nicole was four years old. He had no idea she'd even existed, and still wouldn't know about her, if Heath hadn't contacted him. "Janae, let's not say things we don't really mean."

Was there anger still bubbling inside him? Yes.

Would he allow it to be his focus? No.

He was here now. Janae had welcomed him into her home, albeit reluctantly. Nicole had opened her arms to him, willing to accept the words of her mother, and his place in her life as her father. As of right now, that was the only thing he cared about.

"So, are you going to tell me what's going on with those ladies over there?" Tilting his head towards the women sitting on the other side of the room.

"No," Janae answered shortly.

He wasn't willing to let this go. But he also knew right now wasn't the time to press the issue. Looking over at the little girls getting ready to step on the floor as the recital was about to begin, he smiled at Nicole in her pink tutu. "I know you're hiding something. I don't know what it is, but I do want to find out."

Janae grabbed her bottom lip with her teeth, worrying the flesh, as she seemingly ignored his statement. His eyes continued to watch her as she picked at the seam of her pants as they sat there. He was becoming annoyed at the entire situation. Why wouldn't she tell him what was bothering her and why those women were whispering about her?

"It's nothing, Noah."

"If you say so." Turning his attention back to the front, he settled into the uncomfortable chair and prepared to watch his little girl dazzle him with her stellar ballet moves.

Noah knew he had plenty of time to figure out what was going on with Janae, because he was here until the end. His eyes were glued to the group of children getting into position as their instructor gave them directions. It felt good sitting here with them, doing something so domestic. Things a father would do with his family.

Except his mind was unsettled by the women giving Janae the cold shoulder. Something was fishy about the entire situation and it pissed him off. Small towns held big secrets, but Janae refused to hide away as if they'd done something wrong. Noah was proud of her for holding her head high. Janae's thigh nudged his, bringing his attention back to the tiny dancers. Noah was ready to begin living his new life. He just hoped Janae was ready for what that meant for her and Nicole.

CHAPTER 8

Janae

Clapping her hands loudly as the recital ended, Janae knew her moment of reckoning was coming closer by the minute. She c

ould tell by the glances from the group of women who were more involved in her business than they had a right to be. They were curious about Noah, and they were chomping at the bit to approach her once the children finished.

Throughout the entire hour they'd been sitting there, the women's eyes kept sliding over to Janae and Noah. It was killing them that they didn't know who Noah was. And she could only imagine the myriad of thoughts running through their heads. Screw them. They'd treated her like shit the entire time she'd been bringing Nicole to that studio.

In all honesty, more than half her community treated her like crap on the bottom of their shoe. The hostility stemmed from her own family's church. Janae hated the way they looked at her. The way they judged her. All they saw was a single black mother raising a mixed child on her own. They didn't understand what happened with her and Noah. Nor did they care. All they cared about was telling her how to live her life, and reminding her that she'd somehow failed to live up to some arbitrary expectation they had for her. Fuck them. They weren't the ones who had to live her life. Whatever happened between her and Noah was none of their business, and she wouldn't give them the satisfaction of seeing her crumble again if he left.

Sadness overcame her as she looked at Noah's face as he watched their daughter. She knew she'd been wrong to keep them apart. Stephanie told her repeatedly that it was a bad idea to keep something like this from him. That Noah's reasons for leaving weren't because he didn't care. That his lack of outreach wasn't because she didn't mean anything to him.

At the time, Janae had been too hurt to listen to anything Stephanie had to say. Her only thought was that he'd left her. On her own. Pregnant with his child. With him nowhere around and her taking the burden of their sin on her shoulders alone. It didn't matter if he didn't know she was pregnant. If he'd been here, if he'd never left her in the first place, then he would have known. Things would be different.

But he had, and they weren't.

Janae had her own issues with Noah, but she knew blaming him for not being there wasn't entirely on his shoulders. She had to bear some blame for what she'd done. It was her own actions, or inactions, that had gotten them to this place. She could have fixed this a long time ago. Fear of his reaction to the news of his daughter is what held her back. Now she was paying the price and didn't know how to handle it.

Her daughter's voice caught her ear and brought her attention back to the front of the room.

"Mommy! Did you see?"

Janae looked at her daughter, a smile coming over her face. Opening her arms wide, she waited for the crash of Nicole's little body catapulting into her arms. "I did baby. You did such a good job. I'm so proud of you."

Nicole looked over at Noah, "Daddy! Did you see me?"

Janae's heart stopped at her daughter's loud voice. Nicole had not been quiet when she'd called out to Noah, which was common. But this time, her daughter's voice seemed to boom across the entire studio. Everyone turned their heads to look at the trio. Some with looks of shock on their face. Others with knowing smiles. You could hear a pin drop in the room as everyone realized the father of Janae's child had been sitting there with them the entire time. And that's when the whispers started. She could hear the sound build throughout the room. The whispers. The titters. The questions.

Hanging her head for a second, she took a deep breath. She knew this day was coming but hadn't expected it to happen so soon.

"You okay?" Noah was leaning toward Janae, questions hovering in his eyes.

He was a smart man. He would have noticed a change in the room as soon as Nicole call him daddy. Nodding her head at him, she whispered, "There've been questions."

Noah turned his attention back to their daughter, giving Janae a moment to get her bearings. She could almost guarantee the busybodies would have every detail of this morning out in the street within minutes of leaving the recital.

She was positive her mother would be calling shortly. Did these women have nothing better to do with their lives? They must not if they were always worried about what she was doing and how she was living her life. She'd been under their scrutiny since the moment her stomach began expanding due to her pregnancy, with no sign of a wedding ring on her finger. Everyone wanted to know who the father was. Why hadn't he married her? Why was she here on her own, dealing with this by herself? Had she been abandoned? As if they had a right to do so, they never stopped digging into her life. The innuendo had never been subtle. It was right in her face with every interaction.

She'd been propositioned by more than half of the husbands of each woman sitting in this room today. It sickened her. All of them thinking since she was a single mother, she must be loose and easy. That she would open her legs to anyone with a smile and some slick words. Glancing at the women, she smirked, shaking her head in disgust. If only they knew the tea she could spill. While they sat there looking down their noses at her, judging her for things they knew nothing about, they needed to look at their own homes. Look at their own husbands and fix what was going on in their own homes.

Anger bubbled to the surface when she noticed one woman cut her eyes at her, shaking her head in disgust. She knew exactly what that was all about. The bigotry still running rampant through her own community made her want to scream.

"Need to mind their own damn business," she whispered while gathering their belongings.

If they could guess and spread gossip about Nicole's parentage, they were happy to do so. It gave them a reason to keep Janae's name in their mouth and keep the focus off themselves and their issues. It kept them involved in her life, while ignoring the dust piling up on the skeletons lingering in their closets. It was their way of keeping her in her place by bringing up the age-old topic discussed on the front porches of black families in the South. Did Janae betray her own race? Had she become a bed wench for a white man?

Now they'd seen Noah sitting here with her, and Nicole clearly calling him her dad, it made the situation clear for everyone. Janae had gotten pregnant by a white man, who had not married her, who'd also left her to have a baby and raise her child on her own, and now he was back.

"Are you ready to go?" Noah's voice broke through her internal musings, and she looked over at him with a question on her face.

"What?"

"I said, are you ready to go?" Noah motioned over to Nicole. When Janae looked in her direction, she noticed her daughter standing there patiently. Her ballet slippers shoved into her small backpack, the pink silk laces falling out and dangling toward the floor. Janae was so lost in her own thoughts, she hadn't noticed any of the activity around her.

"Oh. Yes, I'm ready." Noah reached out an arm, resting his hand on her lower back. His touch sent tingles shooting up her spine, her breathing hitched, and her head lifted towards his face. They walked in the direction of their daughter. Standing off to the side with one of her friends, Nicole looked over to them, her face beaming with joy. They'd almost made it when a voice called out to her. She cringed. Things were about to go south in about two-point-five seconds.

"Hey, Janae! Hey girl! What's up? I didn't get to talk to you today. You sat over there all by yourself." The woman looked over at Noah and raised her eyebrows, "Well, not quite by yourself."

Janae didn't want to introduce them, but she knew there was no getting around it. "Hey, Sharon. This is Noah. Noah... Sharon." Her voice lacked friendliness or enthusiasm, but she didn't care at this point. Sharon was only here to start trouble. She was the resident busy body and a member of her family's church.

Even in their teens, when they were in junior high school together, Sharon had been a thorn in her side. Gossip was her middle name. Petty was the name everyone called her—behind her back and in front of her face. No good would come out of this conversation.

Noah reached out to shake Sharon's hand, and the sugary sweet smile she gave him and Nicole, made Janae's skin crawl. She knew that look. Sharon was sizing up Noah to see exactly what he was made of, or trying to at least. Although Sharon claimed to only be about black love, Janae knew she spread her love around to whatever man was willing to take her up on it, whether he be black, brown, white, or tan.

Janae was done playing this childish game. Sharon had her weekly dose of gossip now, so it should feed her dark soul for the next week or so. "Sharon, we have to go. We have some errands to run."

The wicked gleam in the woman's eyes gave Janae all the warning she needed. The next words out of her mouth would not be welcome.

"So, I heard Nicole call Noah daddy. Did I hear that right? Did the prodigal father finally return?"

Anger rose to the surface. Clenching her fist, Janae wanted to knock the smirk off the other woman's face. It would not be okay for her to punch another mother in ballet class. Especially not in front of Noah, or her child. Sighing, she stepped closer to the woman.

"Why do you need to know? That you would ask such a disrespectful question in front of my child doesn't make me happy, Sharon. You should know better than to piss me off." Janae had handed Sharon's ass to her a few times in the past. The woman should know better than to test her, especially in front of Janae's child.

Sharon's shifty eyes looked around the room for an ally. Too bad for her, there was no movement from the peanut gallery. "I was just wondering. I mean, it's been almost five years. No one has seen him before now." Turning fake, sad eyes to look at Noah and Nicole standing off to the side, she shook her head in faux sympathy.

"You have ten seconds to say what you need to say. You're testing my nerves, Sharon. Don't make me embarrass you in front of all these people."

Although her face held a smirk, the snarky woman took a step back. "I mean, it had to be hard all on your own. Well, your parents and the church helped you as much as they could. If you've been hiding a full-grown man—" with this, she looked Noah up and down, from the bottom of his feet to the top of his head, "—while everyone's been supporting you, I think it's important for the church to know. I mean, you did go against God. You lay with a man without the sanctity of marriage. You bore his child." Sharon's lip curled as she looked between Noah and Janae, her eyes shooting fire at the two of them. "That you had a child out of wedlock with a colonizer is gonna break your mother's heart. And you know our families don't roll like that."

Enough! Janae heard all she could stand. Anger and frustration, and yes, shame, rolled through her body. She could feel all the eyes of the women in the room staring at them as Sharon bared Janae's guilt-ridden soul to the masses.

She did have a child out of wedlock. With a white man. She was embarrassed that she'd been a single mother, but she wasn't going to accept the hateful words coming out of Sharon's mouth. And yes, her parents would want to know why he'd come back to town, especially now. But that conversation was between her and her parents. Janae wouldn't hang her head low for living her life.

Noah stood to the side of her, his arms folded over his chest. She could feel the irritation coming off him in waves, even though he hadn't said one word. Looking over to Nicole, she saw her standing a few feet away from them with one of her best friends. The two girls giggling about something as they whispered to each other.

A headache was rapidly building. This is what life had been like for the last four-plus years. Everyone judging. Everyone getting in her face. And now Sharon had the nerve to stand here and lecture her about her what she owed to God, the church, and her parents, as if she had every right to do so. If Janae was such an immoral, godless, loose, race-traitor, then she may as well live up to her reputation.

"Sharon. I've given you more time than intended. Now, I'm going to tell you this only one time. Stay the fuck out my business." The woman in front of her gasped, stepping back. Janae inched closer. "Neither you, the church, nor my parents, get to judge who I sleep with or who I have a child with. The church didn't help me. They judged me. They made me feel less than. As if my child made me unworthy. Unclean. You stand here with that smug look on your face attempting to lecture me about who Nicole's father is? That shit is priceless." Now she was on a roll, and there was no stopping her. "You've had affairs with practically every husband in town. Your own husband can't stand the sight of you. Are your children even his? Because not only does he doubt it, but so does the entire town. Did you know that? Yeah, don't ever judge me, or what goes on in my life. I put up with you and your trifling ways for too long, and now I'm done."

Taking a deep breath, she moved a step back. Straightening her shirt, she pasted a fake smile on her lips. "Now. You can run tell that to whomever you feel needs to know. But know this, don't you ever come at me again with some mess like this. Especially when my child is around. This is your one warning. Don't make me tell you again." Turning to look at Noah, she saw his face still held a hint of annoyance as he continued staring at Sharon standing there. Janae called out to Nicole with her hand outstretched. "Come on Nicole. Let's go, sweetheart. Time to go home."

The three of them walked out of the ballet studio with their heads held high.

Janae wanted to go back inside and slap Sharon upside her head but knew that would be the wrong thing to do. There were a bunch of little girls still standing around. That wasn't something they should see. However, all bets were off if Janae saw Sharon out on the street. She wouldn't hesitate to give her the beat down she deserved. Mumbling to herself, she made her way to Noah's truck. Walking faster than she realized, she didn't slow down until Noah grabbed Nicole up in his arms.

He wanted to know what happened back there, she could tell. "I don't know what's going on in that head of yours, but I need it to stop." Noah gave her a hard look as he continued walking to his truck with Nicole in his arms.

She watched as he quickly made his way over to the vehicle. He and Nicole whispered and laughed as the two of them moved ahead of her. Shaking her head, Janae knew she'd allowed Sharon to get the best of her. She never should've let her get under her skin, but it had become too much. All the tongue wagging and hateful words and judgmental stares had finally pushed her to her limit.

Yes, she hadn't told anyone about Noah. Hell, her parents didn't even know everything that happened between them. She had a right to her own privacy, especially when it came to her child. When she made the decision to keep her daughter, she knew there would be questions. Too many to answer at the time. The thing was, she didn't care then, and she still didn't care four-and-a-half years later. But she was reasonable enough to understand there was someone else involved now.

Noah.

As Nicole got older, Janae knew the issues would continue. People would press and push and ask about her heritage. Janae didn't want her daughter to defend her mother, her father, or the relationship between her parents. It was too much for a child to have to deal with. And since Janae was her mother, she'd never have to. Today would be just the beginning. More people would come with their innuendo. Janae wasn't defeated, but she knew things weren't going to get any easier.

Her phone started to buzz, indicating a call was coming through, and Janae stopped walking. Tilting her back, her face up to the sky, she closed her eyes briefly. She knew exactly who it was even before looking at the screen. It was one of two people. Her mother or her father. Sharon's flapping lips had already started down their path of destruction.

"I knew I should have punched her in the face," she growled under her breath. *Stop being a child, Janae. You knew this day was coming.*

Janae knew Sharon had immediately called or texted the church elders to tell them what she'd seen. That woman had a big mouth. Choosing instead to ignore the call, she allowed her phone to go to voicemail, Janae began marching towards the truck again just as Noah closed the door to the back.

His eyes were harsh. So many thoughts had to be swirling around in his brain. There was no way he hadn't looked at the situation and figured out what was happening. She was almost certain he'd figured out something was wrong in her world. Coming around the front of the truck, Noah stood in front of her. His hands rested on his hips as he silently gazed down at her. Janae felt the urge to shift and move, but knew it was a sign of weakness. Instead, she stood frozen in front of him, waiting for him to confront her with the questions swirling around his brain. She wasn't giving up anything. If he wanted to know what was going on, he could open his mouth.

"Are you going to explain to me what happened in there? Are you going to tell me why that woman felt she could say those things to you? Are you going to tell me why she's claiming you slept with the enemy? That woman called me a colonizer." His last statement ended in a near yell. Noah's chest heaved, his fists were clenched, his lips pressed thin, and his eyes reflecting the storm building inside of him.

The moment of truth had come sooner than she thought. It was time to finally come clean. Her chickens had come home to roost.

CHAPTER 9

Noah

"Is she down for the night?" Noah watched Janae come back into the living room after putting Nicole to sleep.

It allowed her to avoid the conversation they both knew needed to happen. There was too much going on in her world that Noah wasn't aware of, and that worried him. When they'd gotten home from Nicole's ballet class, he focused on spending time with his daughter, enjoying the day getting to know her. They played with dolls, watched several princess movies, and he volunteered to be her jungle gym until she moved on to something else. He was worn out, but this was the happiest he'd been in years.

Looking at the woman walking into the kitchen, and avoiding his gaze, he knew their night was not going to go smooth. Standing, he strolled behind her, not willing to have any more distance between them. Not now. Not tonight.

Coming up behind her as she stood at the kitchen sink, he paused for a moment before pressing his body against hers. Wrapping his arms around her waist, he drew her closer, pulling her back against his chest. Holding her close like this, after all this time, felt right to him. He knew she had every right to push him away and tell him to go pound sand. If she forced him to move his body away from hers, he'd understand because it was what he deserved. Yes, she had every right to tell him all of this, but everything in him hoped and prayed she didn't.

"What are you doing, Noah?" Her body had stilled, but he felt her heavy breaths as her chest rose and fell as his arms wrapped around her warm flesh.

"I've missed you." Even he could hear the agony in his voice. How he managed to leave her in the first place was still beyond him. He'd missed her. Her smile. Her scent. That full laugh that caused her nose to crinkle. Most of all, he'd missed having her in his arms where she belonged.

"There's too much between us now. It's been too long since you left me. Without a backward glance, you disappeared on us."

Noah leaned down, his nose brushing against the side of her neck. His lips trailed soft kisses along her neck and shoulder. Her smooth skin brought back memories of their time together, and his departure. His departure hadn't been planned. When he'd gotten the call to go on a mission, there was no other choice. He'd had to go. They knew the reality of his situation. However, it was fear that kept him away from her for so long. Now that he was back, and realized everything he'd missed, he wasn't willing to walk away. Not again. "No, baby, there's not too much between us. We can get back to where we were. I'm not giving up on us."

Janae's body jerked away from him. Her head turned so she could look him in the face. "Did you forget? You already gave up on us." Closing her eyes, she placed her hands on his chest and pushed. "Let me go," she demanded.

"No."

"Stop Noah. Don't do this to me. You can't just walk back into my life and demand we pick up where we were before. You walked away from me. I've been on my own, depending on myself. I had to be strong for our daughter because you were nowhere to be found."

Noah saw the tears welling in her eyes and jerked back, unwrapping his arms from her waist. Anger coursed through his veins as he looked down at her face. "Don't try to put all this on me. You had a choice as well. You could have called me. You knew where I was and how to find me."

Janae began pacing in front of him, her hands flailing in the air as she mumbled to herself. She was probably trying not to yell loud enough to wake up their daughter. Good. He wanted her angry. He wanted her to let it out. Tell him how they'd gotten to this point. Yes, he'd fucked up, but she'd had his child and never told him. They needed to get to the bottom of this because come hell or high water, he wasn't leaving until he had his woman back, and his daughter by his side.

Her eyes burned with righteous anger as she stared at him. He smirked. *Bring it, baby.*

"That's not fair, Noah. I asked about you every day. Begged Heath to tell me where you were so I could reach you. And know what he told me? I have it memorized since I got the same damn answer every time. He couldn't tell me anything because the information was classified, and you were unreachable. When I tried to go through the base command to get a message to you, they blew me off. Want to know why? I wasn't a relative or spouse. To them, I meant nothing. What else was I supposed to do?" Wetness trailed down her face, coating her cheeks, and dripping onto her shirt. She stood in front of him pleading with him to believe her words, her hands up in supplication.

Neither of them expected her to become pregnant. They'd used precaution. Then again, they were both adults and knew the only way to completely prevent pregnancy was to abstain from sex. But with Janae, there was no way in hell he could have kept his hands off her or not made love to her every chance he got.

If only things could have been different. Then again, those thoughts did nothing to help the situation. At the time, he'd done what was needed. He wouldn't regret his time in the military just because it had taken him away from the woman he loved and his child. Men had to go through it every day, and so did many women.

Even with those rational thoughts going through his head, none of it changed how he felt about the situation. And from the way she was looking at him, he knew he had a long way to go before she trusted him again. Rubbing his hand across his short hair, he turned away from Janae to steady his breathing. Tilting his head back, he closed his eyes for a second, "If I had known, I never would have left. I never would have been gone for so long."

"Then maybe it's a good thing you weren't here. If the only reason you would have stayed is because you found out I was pregnant, I wouldn't have wanted you here. People who stay together just because they have a child... Well, that isn't the way to start a life. I would never want to feel as if I forced you to be with me."

Whipping around, Noah stormed in her direction, coming to stand within a few inches of her. "That's not what I meant, and you know it. I'm just saying. If I had known, I would have been here. I never would have allowed you to go through this on your own. I was off playing the hero to others while you were alone, going through everything by yourself." Lifting his hand to her face, he brushed the back of his fingertips along her cheek. His voice was low. Raw with regret. "You are still so goddamned beautiful."

"Stop saying things like that." Janae turned her head away and tried to move away from him.

"Why? Nothing's changed for me. I still feel the same way about you. You gave me something I was missing. My walking away had nothing to do with you, or what we had together, or the way I felt about you. It had everything to do with me." Cupping her face in his palms, he leaned his head down towards her, "I've missed you, Janae. I thought about you every day that I was away from you. I tried to forget you, tried to overwrite the memories of our time together with other things. I tried to let you go."

"Why?" Her soft lips trembled.

He could tell she thought it was something about her that made him want to pull away. To leave her behind. It wasn't. If only she knew how much life she breathed into him, she'd never question how much she meant to him. His dark and tattered soul needed her. He'd seen too much, done too much, to ever be a truly good man. "Sweetheart, I'm not someone you need in your life."

Her light brown eyes looked up at him, and he could see the hurt reflected in her gaze. It tore him apart. The love he felt for this woman hadn't gone away in the years he'd been gone. He'd done things he wasn't proud of. Things he prayed she'd never find out.

"But I wanted you. I needed you. So many nights I lay in bed, cradling my stomach, praying you'd come back to me. To us. I know what your job is Noah."

"You don't understand," he interjected.

"You're right. I don't."

"I'm not perfect. Never have been. Never will be."

"I never asked for that," she sighed. Glaring at him, her brow crinkled, and her sexy button nose scrunched. "Stop making excuses, Noah. Stop telling me what I want from you and listen to me. You say you're someone I don't need in my life. I'm telling you you're wrong. You chose to give up on us without giving me a chance to accept everything about you, including a job that asked you to kill on command."

His eyes closed to hide the emotions swirling within. He felt close to blurting out everything he'd done since they'd been apart. Every sin. Every transgression. Every person whose life had been snuffed out by his actions or deeds.

He'd honestly thought it had been the best thing for him to walk away. Seeing the effect death had on the family of his fallen comrades, he swore he never wanted to put someone through that. The utter devastation that happened to a family when a fallen Marine or Sailor came home in a box. When the husband was no longer there to tell his wife and kids everything would be okay. When the uncertainty of how they died tore at their soul as they wondered if their loved one suffered, or if they called out for their wife and child. He never wanted that life for Janae.

This woman was the love of his fucking life, and for that reason alone, he knew he was no good for her. It wasn't that he couldn't love her the way she needed to be, because he could. It was the possibility of his death, of leaving her on her own, that wouldn't allow him to take the gift she'd presented to him.

Now he back where he'd first began. Here he stood, observing Janae standing just feet away from him and he knew, without a doubt, he was fucked.

Taking a few steps closer to her, he took a deep breath. "I'm not going anywhere, and I'm not going to give you another reason to doubt my feelings for you, or just how much I want to be in Nicole's life." Wrapping his arms around her waist to pull her close, he lowered his head and gazed into her eyes. "Some things were going on at the time, and I felt it was the best decision for both of us. That was the wrong thing to do. I get that now. But believe me, it had nothing to do with you, or what we shared. Do you still... Do you still love me?"

Janae closed her eyes. He felt her breathe deep as she avoided his gaze.

"Answer me, Janae. I need to know I'm not in this alone."

Eyes still closed, Janae's voice whispered up to him. "I've never stopped loving you. When you left, I almost died. I stopped eating. Stopped wanting to be here. I didn't understand what happened to make you cut me off the way you did. Every day, I questioned what I had done wrong to make you go away."

Noah's heart hurt at her words. He'd been a fool. Although her eyes opened, her gaze was off to the side.

"I was so devastated when you left. It was as if you'd died. That you'd been taken away from me without warning, and I had no time to tell you goodbye. At least not the way I wanted to. Finding out I was pregnant with your child was what brought me back to the living. Our baby was the only reason I got out of bed in the morning. Why I made myself eat. Our baby. We'd created a miracle together." Pausing, she finally turned her gaze to his. "No matter how angry I was with you, I never stopped loving you."

CHAPTER 10

Noah

Noah dipped his head, capturing her lips with a strong kiss. His tongue made its way into her mouth, dueling with hers as he tried to convey his feelings with this one sensual act. Pressing against her body, his cock thickened as he situated his large form between her soft thighs. Although they were still standing in the kitchen, he wasn't allowing this moment to get away from him. He needed to be close to her. His body had missed her. His heart craved her.

Her soft lips moved along his as she kissed him just as deeply. Soft hands caressed his body from his side to his chest to his shoulders, until her arms wrapped around him, gripping him along his back, just under his shoulder blades. One leg lifted, attempting to wrap itself around his waist as her moans filled the kitchen. A testament to how much each of them was enjoying this. Pulling away for just a second, he looked down into her eyes and a smile came over his face.

Her eyes were dazed, glazed over with lust. Her soft lips were swollen from the pressure of his kiss. Long, deep sighs filled the room, bringing back memories of their long nights and days when they were together in bed. He wanted nothing more than to be by this woman's side for the rest of his days. If he had to spend the rest of his life making up for the mistake of leaving her, he would. No one was taking his family away from him again.

"Let me stay the night," he pleaded.

"That might not be a good idea. What if Nicole finds you here? She knows you're her father, but she still so young. I don't want to confuse her." Her hand came up to rub along the back of his neck, it had always been her favorite activity when they were together. After they'd finished making love, she'd rub her hands along his skin as if trying to memorize the feel of his body.

"I don't want to confuse her, but I don't want to leave. Not tonight. Now that I have you in my arms again, I don't want to let you go. Just give me a chance to make everything up to you. Let me show you how much I want you. That I need you."

Janae stood there looking at him for a few long seconds. He almost smiled as he watched her. His woman was trying to make up her mind about him. She was trying to decide the best thing for them. He knew she still had her doubts about him. Based on his past behavior, he knew she questioned if he was someone who could stick it out when the road got tough. He knew she had reason to doubt him. He wouldn't blame her for that. Not tonight. Not ever. Not when the other half of his heart slept in a princess bed down the hallway. She had every right to protect her daughter—their daughter—from heartache.

The only thing he wanted right now, no—what he *needed*—was to be balls deep inside of her. Needed to feel her tight pussy as he thrust inside her. Her slick channel contracting around his hard, thick cock. Noah ached with the need to claim his woman. It had been too long. His desire for her was practically clawing at him to be set free.

"Come on, Sweetheart. You're killing me here."

Janae grabbed his hand as she began walking out of the kitchen and down the hallway to her bedroom. They stopped for a moment so Janae could check on Nicole sleeping in her room. When she came back into the hallway, she softly closed the door. They both turned to continue the trek down the hallway to Janae's bedroom.

Once inside, Noah couldn't keep his hands off her body. Rushing over to Janae, he scooped her in his arms. Her legs wrapped around his waist, her warmth resting on top of his pulsating dick. His mouth took hers in a ravenous kiss as he pressed the two of them together. Getting as close as possible, without actually fucking.

"I missed this," he whispered, moving his kisses from her lips to her neck.

"I did, too," Janae moaned. Her body squirmed on top of his, pressing her body closer to his. "The bed. Take me to the bed."

"As you wish." Walking over to the king-size bed situated in the center of the room, Noah lay her down on her back on top of the quilt. His hands began roaming over her body, reacquainting himself with the landscape of her body that he'd missed for so long. Every valley and crevice had been his to explore for so long. It felt like coming home. Noah's dick continued to press against the zipper of his jeans, almost becoming painful in his need to be inside of his woman.

His long fingers began removing her shirt from her body, "Lift your arms." Once she did, he quickly removed the shirt from her body and flung it across the room. Just the sight of her breasts made his mouth water.

He longed to feel the soft flesh in his mouth, her hard nipples brushing against his soft tongue. Lifting the bra away from her breasts without unsnapping it, he leaned down and captured one nipple in between his lips. Suckling the turgid flesh, he bit down lightly with his teeth as she squirmed underneath him. He could feel the precum leaking from the tip of his cock, as his hips began thrusting forward and back, mimicking the motion of making love to his woman.

"Please, Noah," she pleaded, licking her plump lips.

Leaning over her, he peered into her eyes before dipping his head to run his tongue over the lingering wetness on her mouth. *I'll never get tired of looking at her.*

Moving his mouth from her wet nipple, he grinned at her. "There's no need to beg baby. I'm here for as long as you want me. I'm not leaving you again."

Even in the haze of lust, Noah noticed Janae didn't respond to his declaration. She simply stared at him before she smiled seductively. "You have too many clothes on," she purred.

He didn't need another hint. He began tearing off his clothes in record fashion. As each item was removed, he flung it somewhere in the room. He'd worry about picking them up after he satisfied his need to fuck his woman all night. She'd granted him this night, but that didn't mean her bedroom would be open to him tomorrow. Noah would have to make sure she remembered just how good they were together.

Within seconds, he was bare-assed naked standing in front of her. His thick cock was leaking precum as he stared down at her. "Your turn," he demanded. It was becoming too much. If he didn't get inside her soon, he would lose his damn mind.

Standing from the bed, Janae placed her hands on the waistband of her pants. Noah couldn't resist reaching out to help her. Her soft giggle sounded in the room, but he didn't care if he looked desperate with need. All that mattered was getting her naked. Pride and ego had been left outside in the hallway to languish while he got his fill. Quickly removing the material from her body, he flung it over his shoulder.

They stood in the middle of her bedroom; their naked bodies pressed together. His dick was growing rapidly from being so close to his desire. "Are you on birth control?"

Although he asked, he didn't really care. He wanted her something fierce, and he didn't want to wait. If their coming together meant she would have another child, he was okay with that possibility. Hell, he was almost hoping his seed would take root inside her body again. He'd give anything to see her stomach expand with his baby growing healthy inside her body. He would be by her side this time, removing any question about his commitment to her, or to their baby. If necessary, he would respect the need for birth control if she wanted it, but that wasn't his focus. The one thing he cared about most was being with Janae; reconnecting with the only woman who'd ever had his heart.

"Yes, I take the shot every three months." Was it his imagination, or did her soft voice hold a note of regret?

Something within Noah rebelled at the thought of her body blocking them from creating another miracle. Plus, they weren't together so why the need for precaution? He knew it was a stupid thought, but he couldn't help it. To him, it meant there was a possibility that someone else may have wanted to be where he was right now.

Looking down at her, he bared his teeth in a feral growl. He knew his jealousy was unwarranted. He was the one lying in bed with her tonight, and that was all he needed to know. But just the thought of her being with someone else this way made his heart clench with pain. Made him want to stake his claim. Made him desire to imprint on her as he forced her to remember how good they were together. How much they'd loved each other once.

Grabbing her chin in one strong hand, he held her face in position as she looked into his eyes. He needed her to hear his words. "There's no one else but me from this point forward. I fucked up. I admit it. But you... you and Nicole are every—" he paused, clearing his throat. "I'm not leaving you again. So, if there was someone else who thought to be in my spot, they're shit out of luck."

"There's no other man." Janae dipped her gaze.

He knew it wasn't the full truth but wasn't willing to go down that road tonight. "Look at me," he demanded. "This is not the end. One time with you will never be enough for me. No other man will ever be able to take my place. You can deny it all you want, but you and I both know it's true. I'm the only man who knows how to give you what you need. My touch is what your body craves. My hard dick stroking inside your warm, wet pussy as you scream out your orgasm and your juices flow from your body, is what we both need."

"Noah..." she gasped. He smiled, knowing he was getting to her. That she was remembering all those days and nights they'd spent together.

"I'll never stop wanting you. Never stop fucking you. Never stop licking your pussy and tasting your juices as you drip all over my tongue. That's what I want from this day forward. You and me."

Janae rested her forehead on his chest when he finished speaking. His large hands rubbed along her luscious body. There were a few more curves than he remembered, but they just made her even sexier. Grabbing a handful of her thick ass, he pulled her closer to his rigid flesh.

"Baby. Give me what I need. What we need," he implored.

Lifting her head, she gazed into his eyes. Dropping her eyes to his thick, straining cock, she reached one hand down to graze the tip. Gathering a drop of his precum on her finger, she lifted the digit to her mouth and sucked the cream away.

Noah moaned low in his throat. "You're killing me, baby. You're mine, Janae. You know that, right?"

They stared at each other for a long heartbeat before she wrapped her arms around his neck. "If you want me back, you have to earn me."

"I plan to. I'm sorry I hurt you. Sorry I left you to deal with everything on your own. But I'm back now. With you. Leaving you wasn't the answer. I've missed out on building a life together. Being without you was like ripping out my heart. If I have to earn your trust, your love, I'll do whatever it takes."

CHAPTER 11
Janae

Janae gave a single nod as her breath lodged in her throat. "I need you, Noah." Looking down at him, she licked her lips in anticipation. The man was fine as hell. She'd often wondered how she'd gotten so lucky.

His stomach was flat, lean, corded with muscles. Tattoos covered most of his stomach and chest, and it made him look even more badass than he already was. Colors blended into one another, until many of the images were indiscernible, except for a dagger, dripping with blood. It looked as if it was painted over another image. She pressed her lips to his chest. "You're driving me crazy."

Noah fisted her hair, forcing her to look at him. "I haven't started."

Delicious shivers rippled up her spine. Her clit throbbed as Noah held her tight before whispering his command.

"Show me where you need me."

Janae swallowed down a breath. Shakily, she spread her folds, wet to the touch. His gaze flickered, hardened.

"Keep it just like that for me, Sweetheart."

She did. Janae kept herself open for him even as her breath hitched then ceased altogether when he fisted his cock. Her eyes latched on to the sight and she whimpered. She missed this. Missed him. Just the thought of him sliding his hardened flesh inside her body, increased her need for him. Making love to Noah had changed her forever. The slide of his thick cock as he took her to the pinnacle and back. Those large hands of his gripping her body tight against his hard form. He never allowed her to leave the bed until she had at least two full-blown, body-arching orgasms. Low moans began releasing from her lips as she watched him stroll closer to her. A sliver of fear and desire nestled in her belly. Janae couldn't help but think he was going to rip her apart, it had been so long, but she didn't care. Despite the fear, she couldn't help but look her fill or stop the rush of moisture trickling on to her fingers. Thick, reddened veins ran along the length of him. The swollen crown was thicker than the already trunk-like base.

Moisture dripped from the slit and slid below the engorged rim. Heat raced up Janae's face when more liquid spilled from the crown. Unconsciously, she wet her lips.

"You're licking your lips." His lips eased into a tender smile as he moved between her legs. The warm tip pressed sensually against her vulva.

"Curious." Janae whimpered. "I want to taste you."

"N-next time." His voice sounded strained. "Can't let myself think about those pretty lips wrapped around me. Not right now."

"Fuck me," she begged.

"Are you wet for me, baby? No other man can give you what I can." Noah moved down her body, pressing small kisses along her skin before placing his face near her wet opening. His tongue pressed against her hardened clit and her body jerked. "Mmmmm," he moaned just before wrapping his lips around her nubbin and sucking the flesh into his warm mouth. Her toes curled as his hands pushed her legs wider, opening her body to his searing gaze. "Fuck, you taste so damn good. Janae, look at me."

Opening her eyes, she caught his gaze. No words could escape her mouth. She was a bundle of nerves, and everything in her prayed Noah would continue.

"Don't take your eyes off me." He smiled. "Nod, if you understand."

Head bobbing as if on a string, she finally managed to whisper, "Please."

At her plea, Noah's head dipped again to her quivering pussy. His mouth latched onto her flesh with enough force, she released a squeal in shock. Her hands lifted and covered her mouth to silence the sound.

"No. Look at me," Noa demanded from his position between her legs. Once she placed her gaze on his, he went back to work.

Tears formed in her eyes from the sheer magnitude of the feelings coursing through her body. Even if she wanted to, she wouldn't have been able to stop her hips from rotating and lifting.

More.

She wanted more. His lips and tongue brought her so much pleasure. Within minutes, her body was catapulting toward orgasm. Stomach clenching, toes curling, her mouth opening in a silent scream, her release rushed over her like a tsunami. Did Noah give her a break? No. The man kept licking and sucking and kissing as she went through several aftershocks, her body jerking, and wetness falling from her eyes.

"No more," she begged. Her voice was raw and throaty from the strain of holding back her screams. The intensity of her release made her want to curl up in a ball and cry her heart out. She wouldn't though. Noah was in bed with her after all these years. This was one opportunity she wouldn't let pass her by.

"You want this? Me?" Noah licked his lips as he shifted his body, aligning it with hers as he lay between her legs.

"I've always wanted you."

Noah positioned his thick cock at her entrance and began to sink inside her. She moaned in both pleasure and pain. Her body was still clenching, recovering from her release, and Noah wasn't a small man. She welcomed the burn as he claimed her body once again.

He drew in a ragged breath. He stopped, letting out a hoarse grunt.

Janae gasped in return as he grabbed her ass and shoved into her. His lips swallowed her cry. He rained kisses along her face. "Shhhh, baby. I had to do that. You're so tight it would have taken forever to get inside you." He used his thumb to brush away a teardrop at the corner of her eye. She hadn't realized she'd been crying. He began fucking her in a slow rhythm, plunging inside her with long strokes.

Janae bit her lips, feeling her walls adjust to the hard cock moving so deep inside. "Feels so good."

With long steady thrusts, Noah drove deeper and deeper inside her. A muffled cry tore from the back of her throat. Janae raised her hips in wanton abandon. She was lost in the sensation of being connected with this man.

"Oh, God, Janae. I can't slow down, baby." His face became harsh, and the hand around her waist tightened. Over and over again, he pounded into her. Janae knew there was no going back. Not even an oncoming train could have slowed them down.

She gripped the sheets, the pillows, Noah's skin. Whatever was within her grasp to try and brace herself for the sensations rolling through her. "Then d-don't. Don't ever stop."

His eyes darkened. She could hear his breathing grow ragged. "You like this?"

She clenched her muscles around him again. "Yes!"

Noah slowed, then sped up his thrusts. White-hot pleasure wended itself around her, burning to a fevered pitch. "Oh God," she whispered heatedly. Her body shook all over, skin tingling.

"Beg me to stop. Tell me to pull out before I completely lose my mind."

Janae moved her lips, yet the only sound she could manage was a long moan that made his eyes go slant.

"Say it," he urged. "Tell me I'm not allowed to come inside you."

Her head thrashed. She couldn't say what he wanted her to. No, she had her own response. "Yes. Yes, Noah. You can. Just stay...inside me." Wave after wave of pleasure shot through her entire body as her channel tightened around his thick cock.

He was watching her, his eyes intent and focused on her as her body quivered and tiny gasps escaped from her lips. "My Janae," he groaned. Suddenly she saw him stiffen. A split second later she felt jets of hot semen pouring into her.

Janae flushed. She could feel his eyes on her as her body wrung the seed from his shaft. Noah's lips turned at the corners, a tender smile. He slowed to a languid pace. When Noah finally stopped and pulled back, Janae still couldn't catch her breath. She felt her lower lips pulsating, begging for more. Everything was so wet and throbbing, she didn't know what to do.

After a few minutes, Noah separated from her body and went to the bathroom to grab a warm towel. He took his time wiping her body down, cleaning her body. She heard him reenter the bathroom before turning off the light and walking back toward the bed. Janae managed to ease herself upright and settled her eyes on a scene she could hardly believe. Noah stood, inches from her, stroking his massive shaft and licking his lips as if still savoring her essence. His skin glistened in semi-darkness, each muscle all but dancing as he moved.

"You ready for me again?" he asked, stroking the full length of his rapidly hardening member.

Janae nodded. Then she sucked in a breath and braced herself. Noah moved his hips closer to her wet pussy, pushing himself deeper and deeper. With each stroke, she yelped and encouraged him to do more.

"Fuck me harder!" she demanded. "Right there, baby. Right there, Noah."

A thin layer of perspiration appeared on his skin. Noah continued to move his hips, stroking her insides. As Janae's eyes focused in on his, she felt the power of his steel-like shaft. It was so hard; and at this moment, she decided, Noah's dick inside of her was the most wonderful feeling in the world.

She sucked in a breath and closed her eyes. Before she could say anything, he repositioned his body, leaning back on his knees. Holding her by the waist, he aligned her body with his, spreading her wide as her legs wrapped around his waist. "This is what I really want." In one fluid motion, he slid back inside her hot wetness, so deep 'til there was no space between them. Her wetness allowed him to slide in with relative ease.

Her head fell to his shoulders.

"So sweet. So good," he whispered.

Janae's arms tightened around his back, and her hard nipples pressed against his chest.

Noah dipped his head and lifted one supple breast. His mouth closed over the delicious peak. His hand rose up to knead her breast, and Janae sighed his name. Noah moaned deep in his throat as he suckled her flesh. The deep, growly sound, so ripe with need, went straight to her core. He freed her breast from his large hand, gathered a fistful of hair around his fingers and plunged to the hilt. In and out, each plunge harder than the last. Her sex clenched, gripping him tight, her liquid heat flowing from her body, coating the thick flesh entering and exiting her body. Ecstasy rolled through her body in waves as he pushed her legs back, her feet resting on his shoulders. Her mouth opened in a silent scream as Noah's every thrust threatened to shatter her soul.

"Goddamn, baby. You feel so good," Noah grunted.

Janae wiggled her hips and rode him hard. She twisted to the left, lifting her hips, and ground her body against his. She savored the feeling of his hips driving forward; pushing deeper and deeper inside her. "Fuck. Right there, baby. Oh yes!" She moaned loudly as her body continued to slide against his.

"You like it?" he asked. "I wanna give it all to you," he whispered. "I'm so sorry, baby. Never giving you up again. I can't. I won't."

Janae wiggled her hips some more. "You'd better not. Oh, Noah. Please," she whimpered.

"Take it, girl. Handle all this dick. It belongs to you," he moaned.

"Oh, shit!" Janae screamed. Her eyes rolled back. Her mouth flew open. "Oh shit, I'm about to come, baby." Janae couldn't fathom what she was doing. The only thing she could focus on was the sensation. The feeling. The utter rapture.

"Take it. Take all of me inside you," he said with a deep groan.

Janae grabbed his neck and pulled him closer, unable to hold on any longer. She came hard and fast, exploding her juices all over his massive member. Her clit tingling, Janae leaned back to look at Noah.

"You didn't finish." Her voice was hoarse due to the rawness of her throat.

"Nah, that was all about you," he answered.

"Well, that's not gonna work at all," Janae pouted. She pushed against his chest and turned around. "Come on, baby. I know how much you like it." Before he could respond, Janae moved onto her knees and hiked her hips upward. Without hesitation, Noah moved between her legs and entered her with such force, she had to press down further into the mattress to take the full impact of each stroke.

"Yes. Come for me baby," she mewled.

They moved at a steady pace, with an upbeat rhythm. Janae couldn't believe this was happening. As Noah's thickness slid in and out of her with great ease, she got worked up all over again. Soon, a tingling sensation began at the bottom of her feet and started to work its way up her legs. "Oh, fuck," she cried.

She felt the tiny tremors rolling off his frame, the sound of his teeth gnashing followed by low moans. His hips worked furiously, determined to push them beyond the brink of ecstasy. Noah grabbed her breasts in his hands, lifting her body to an upright position. He pulled her close to him, her back pressed against his chest as he stroked, his hips punching forward as they both grunted with their oncoming release. Their bodies entwined, Noah released one breast to grab her chin and turn her face to the side. He captured her lips between his own in a hard, searing kiss as he came apart, spilling warmth deep inside her. Even when the aftershocks subsided and the ticking of the wall clock sounded in her ears, the fear Janae expected to feel, failed to return.

He hugged Janae close and she exhaled. This is what she'd missed. This feeling of contentment flowing through her brought tears to her eyes.

"Damn girl. You and me... together again. Baby, we're about to make some new memories this weekend."

All she could do was smile. This, she decided, was just the kind of excitement she needed.

He buried his face in the side of her neck and hugged her close. Janae smiled, a giggle fighting to escape. He kissed the side of her neck. She turned her head, kissing his bare shoulder. This was heaven. Her body was on cloud nine. Even with that, she wanted more.

"I love you, Janae."

She didn't respond, but she lifted her head to his, catching his lips between her own. Those lips brought her so much pleasure. Soft. Warm. Responsive.

"I love you so damn much," he stated again as they broke apart.

His words were suddenly drowned by a slow ardent kiss as if she were learning the taste of him for the first time. She raised her head from their kiss and gave him a long look, her eyes softening as she stared at him. She hoped he got the message she was sending.

Forgiveness.

She felt his pulse increase as their hands began to roam along naked skin. His cock hardened again, thickening against her soft stomach. There was need reflected in his eyes. She knew her gaze reflected the same message. *I want you.*

CHAPTER 12
Noah

Noah walked into his bland hotel room the next morning. Looking around the space, he snorted derisively. This room was nothing like Janae's home. At her place, it was warm, homey, welcoming. When he left her this morning, everything in him wanted to crawl back in bed and lay beside her. Last night had been everything he could have hoped for. Being with her, sinking inside of her warm body, and loving her all night. That's what he'd missed during the last few years.

Sitting on the edge of his bed, he placed his forearms on his thighs as he thought about everything that happened in the past few days. He'd discovered he had a child, realized the woman he loved all those years ago, still loved him in return, and wanted to change his entire life to be with them. The only problem was, his life today was still the same as it was back then. Nothing had changed for him. He would still have to go away on missions, and his life was constantly in danger. There was still the possibility he'd go on a mission and never return. Not of his own choosing, but due to an enemy bullet.

How could he put Janae and Nicole through something like that? That was the reason he'd left in the first place. His life was not easy. His world was hard. There were times when men he'd known for years held off on getting married, raising a family, only to get to a point when they felt things were moving in the right direction. They'd finally make a choice to open themselves up to the future they'd been so afraid of, only to leave their wife a widow and their child without a father.

He was one of those men, or at least he had been before this weekend. But now, everything had turned on its head. A ding alerted him of a text message coming through. It was from Janae.

"Good morning."

A broad smile came over his face as he looked at her message. *"Good morning, Beautiful,"* he texted back.

"I was sorry you left before I woke up."

He didn't want to leave but had to follow the rules. *"I didn't want to leave. But we agreed, it was best not to confuse Nicole."*

"Still, I missed not having you by my side when I woke up this morning."

"One day we'll be able to fix that. What are you up to today?"

Noah looked at his phone as he waited for Janae to respond to his question. He hoped she would say nothing. He wanted to invite himself over to her house to spend more time with her and Nicole. Even if she said they already had plans, he would be at her house this afternoon, enjoying her company, getting to know his daughter better. Maybe life had given him a second chance. He walked away from her once, and now he had an opportunity to start over. Her response finally came through.

"Church."

Noah's brow worked in confusion. Janae's one-word response raised all types of red flags. *"Going to call you."* Dialing her number, he stood from the bed and began pacing as he waited for her to pick up. As soon as she answered, he jumped in, "Do you not want to go to church?"

"It's not that I *don't* want to go."

Noah heard her sigh on the other side of the line and knew there was more to the story. "Okay. Then what's the problem?"

She sighed again before answering his question. "After yesterday's confrontation with Sharon, I'm positive we'll be the number one topic of the church busybodies. Everyone will want to know just who you are, where you came from, and why you're here. I don't want to deal with the questions or the innuendo. It's no one's business who the father of my child is."

He wished a motherfucker would say another word to Janae about him or their daughter in his presence. "No, it isn't. You dealt with this on your own for too many years. Why do you think it's an issue today?" Noah continued to pace. He knew why today was so different for Janae. Only thing is, he wanted her to say it. He needed her to admit things had changed now that he'd returned. It wasn't like he was going away anytime soon.

He knew she probably had a small amount of doubt and concern about their future. It would take time for her to settle into their new way of living. He would prove that he wasn't going anywhere. That he was truly meant to be with her and Nicole. While he sure as hell didn't expect to live in Jacksonville for the rest of his life, Noah hoped he'd be able to convince Janae that moving to Northern Virginia was in the best interests of their small family.

Janae's defeated tone pulled him back to the conversation. "You just don't understand. If only you knew how much I had to put up with from those people in that church. All the people who judged me. The ones who questioned my morals under a veil of saving my soul. I could almost feel the anger and disappointment they sent my way simply because I was an unwed mother. It almost broke me."

Noah's stomach clenched at her words. He could almost feel how much it hurt her to go through this alone. "What time is church?"

"Why?"

"Because I'm coming with you."

"No, no, no. We're not doing this today. I don't want you to be the focus of their attention. I know how to handle then. If anyone comes to me with any stupid comments, I can ignore them. I've done it before. It's okay Noah, you don't have to rescue me today."

Noah was already looking through his suitcase to see if he had anything that would be acceptable for Sunday church. "No, Janae. I'm not letting you face any of this alone. Not anymore. What time should I pick up you and Nicole?"

"You're not going to let this go?" Janae's soft laughter came through the line. He smiled, even if she couldn't see him. Noah was determined to claim his family. If the first step to doing that was walking into the church where she'd been judged for years, chin held high, holding on to both the woman he loved and his perfect little girl, then that's what he'd do. He knew what people must be thinking, but he'd debunk that idea today. Noah wasn't ashamed of them and would never deny them. Not ever. Anyone who had a problem with him being in their lives, could deal with him.

"Fine. Be here at eleven. We'll be ready to go."

"I'm looking forward to it." He laughed a little, because he knew there was no way in hell he was ready for whatever was about to come their way. If he could fake it 'til they made it, the sooner they could put this behind them.

"I'm sure Nicole will be happy to have her daddy sitting next to her during service. Don't be surprised if she tries to show you off to everyone. When she woke up this morning, she was asking for you."

Noah's heart clenched. That Nicole was looking for him, asking where he was, did something to the jagged parts of him. At one point in his life, he thought he didn't have enough to love for anyone other than himself. Now he knew just how wrong he was.

He cleared the lump from his throat. "And I can't wait to see her either. Janae, you have no idea how glad I am to hear that she's asking for me. Other than my parents, I don't think I've ever had someone to love me unconditionally. Nicole has given me that."

Silence met his statement from the other side of the line. Noah wondered what was going on, "Janae?"

"Noah. You had someone else who loved you unconditionally. You just didn't know it, or you were too afraid to face it."

Noah didn't know what to say in response. Love usually came at a price.

There was always give and take, no matter how much people tried to deny it. Every woman he'd been with, other than Janae, wanted him for their own reasons, and they didn't always jive with his own. They wanted him for the prestige because he was a Navy SEAL, or because he was a military man, or because he knew how to make them scream his name in the bedroom. Or at least they thought he could because of the way he looked. There was always something they wanted from him, and their emotions and feelings for him always came with a price tag attached.

Janae's soft voice broke through his internal musings. "It's okay Noah. We both know you didn't understand what I felt for you. I think that was part of the reason you decided to leave. Because you were unsure of what I wanted from you, of what I needed from you. But now that you're back and you know about Nicole, we need to figure out our next steps. Last night was—wonderful. But I don't know if we should have a repeat performance before we decide what we're going to do next."

Noah immediately responded to her statement, "No, Janae. You don't get to pull away from me. Last night was exactly what we needed. I've been away from you and Nicole for too long. You don't get to tell me I can't be with you when I've told you just how much I need you in my life. You wanted me as much as I wanted you. Don't try and end us now." Noah knew exactly what Janae was doing. She was trying to put him in a box, push him away in some warped attempt to protect her and Nicole. It wasn't going to happen. He wouldn't allow it.

"Noah, that's not what I meant. I'm just saying, maybe we need to think about if we should continue what we're doing. Nicole will be confused when she wakes up one day and you're no longer here. She will be heartbroken. And what am I supposed to tell a four-year-old little girl when the daddy she just found decides this life isn't for him and returns to the one he had before he met her? One that doesn't include her. I just think... maybe we should think about this a little bit more."

"Janae," his whispered harshly. Noah was seething. He didn't know why she was doing this. Well, maybe he did, but he really didn't give a shit. This wasn't fair to him or Nicole. Hell, it wasn't fair to Janae as well.

He wasn't going down without a fight. He'd only left her a few hours ago, and here she was trying to put up a wall between them.

"I'll be there in less than an hour. You don't have to be dressed, but I'm coming there to be with you and Nicole. If you think I'm not going to be with you and Nicole, you're out of your damn mind. Whatever you need from me to help you understand that I'm here for the long haul, I'll give it to you. I'm here, sweetheart, and I'm not going anywhere."

Noah heard Janae practically growl on the other side of the line. Coming back into her life and taking a caveman approach was not the way to win her over to his side. He knew that and would prefer to take his time wooing her all over again, but something about this entire situation rubbed him raw.

Not only was Janae trying to force him away, but she seemed almost afraid to be seen with him in public. He wondered about the incident yesterday and what the lady said to them at the ballet studio. That she'd betrayed her race. That her parents and their church had supported her even when they didn't have to. Was there something more going on and Janae wasn't telling him? She'd already admitted how she'd been treated—ostracized—because she a single, unwed mother. When Nicole was born, and her mixed-race heritage became known, did it become worse?

"Well, if you're going to be this stubborn about it, come on over. But I'm trying to warn you, this is not going to be a walk in the park."

"It doesn't matter," Noah responded. "They just need to see that I'm with you. I'm the one by your side, and I'm happy as fuck to be there. If they have a problem with what we have between us, they can come directly to me. Now, get your ass outta bed, get our daughter up, and I'll be there within the hour with breakfast."

"Has anyone told you how bossy you are?"

He laughed. It was about time she recognized that. "Yup. All the time."

Janae laughed into the phone. "Boy, you're a damn mess. Bye, Noah."

"See you soon, Beautiful."

Noah ended the call with Janae and threw his phone on the bed. In a hotel room silent for a few minutes thinking about everything happening in his life. No one, especially him, would have expected that he would be a father one day.

His parents would be happy to find out about his new family. They'd almost lost hope that he'd settle down with a good woman. Lifting his head, he realized there was one more call to make. How would he tell his parents he had a four-year-old daughter he'd just met? Rubbing a hand down his face, he sighed deeply. No need to put the conversation off any longer. He owed them the courtesy of telling them about their grandchild.

His mother would probably cry. His father would tell him how disappointed he was. Noah understood both of those emotions. He was disappointed in himself. He'd always been the one in control, the one who lived his life with structure and purpose. Exactly the way he wanted it.

He was a protector. The one who looked after everyone else. He'd failed to protect Janae from the hurtful rumors swirling around her. His failure to confront his fear had put Janae in an untenable situation. In his quest to protect himself from hurt, and Janae from the heartache of losing him to the harsh reality of combat, Noah hadn't looked after the people who mattered most to him.

Forty-eight hours.

Such a short time when he thought about it, but in only forty-eight hours, he knew he would give his life to protect his little girl. She was a part of him. The best part of him. And if she were the only thing left of him once his maker called him home, she would be the best thing he could offer to this world.

Looking at the clock, he picked up his phone. Noah sat in one of the chairs sitting around the tiny table in his room and dialed the number he knew by heart. He settled back as the phone rang a few times. Then his mother picked up.

CHAPTER 13
Noah

"Hey, Mom." Noah took a deep breath. This next part would not be easy.

"Hey, Noah. How's it going, sweetheart? We haven't heard from you in a while."

"Well, Mom, that's why I'm calling. Is Dad around?" Noah waited while she called his father over to the phone. Since it was Sunday, he was probably messing around in their garage. His dad had taken up the hobby of building cars and airplanes since his retirement. About three months after he hung up his tie for good, his mother told Noah his father was bored out of his mind and bothering her a bit too much.

As a result, she forced him to find a hobby to keep him busy and out of her hair. His father had fought it tooth and nail until his mother forced him to be in the garage for at least two hours each day before he could come out. At the time, his dad grumbled and mumbled about his mother being a bit too bossy. After a month or so, his father began staying in the garage longer and longer. Until one day his mother had to go and pull him out, forcing him to eat dinner.

Noah hoped one day he and Janae would get to that point. They'd be so comfortable with each other, their entire lives revolved around making each other comfortable, keeping each other sane, and making sure each one had a hobby they enjoyed.

"Hey son," his father announced through the phone. His mother must have put them on speaker so they could both talk to him at the same time.

"Hey, old man," Noah responded, a smile on his face. "I've got some news for you." Noah heard his mother's gasp and knew she was thinking the worst.

"Oh, Noah! What's going on? What's happened? Are you hurt?"

Taking a deep breath, Noah continued. "No, ma'am. Everything's fine. But I do have some news for you. It's good news, or at least I hope you'll think it is." Deciding it was best to just get the words out, he continued. "You're grandparents."

He forged ahead with the story, not giving them a chance to interrupt. "I have a little girl. Four years old. She and her mom live in Jacksonville, North Carolina. She's the most beautiful and perfect little girl I've ever seen. She has her momma's smile, but my eyes. I've spent the past two days getting to know her."

His father's voice broke through his ramblings. "What do you mean you have a little girl? Did you say she's four?"

"Yes, she's four-and-a-half, to be exact."

"Noah, you have a four-year-old daughter, and we're just now finding out about her? Why didn't we know about her years ago? Son, what aren't you telling us?"

Leave it to his dad to get to the real issue. Closing his eyes for a moment, he knew this is where the disappointment would come in. "Because I just found out about her this weekend." A small cry from his mother almost broke his heart. He could only imagine what was going through her head, but he had to get it out.

"Her mother was someone I met six years ago when I was on temporary duty in North Carolina. I left, allowed my job to get in the way, and broke her heart. What I didn't know at the time is that she was pregnant with my child. I'm not sure if she knew either, but it doesn't matter. There's so much to say, and I don't know where to start. The one thing I do know is that I have to fix it." Noah knew his parents would expect nothing less from him.

"Oh my," his mother whispered.

"Her name is Nicole. She looks like me, only a prettier version. She's smart, sassy, she takes ballet lessons on the weekend, and she's already accepted me as her dad. Her mother never hid who I was from her. Told her my job was dangerous. That I had to live far away from them because I had to protect our country from the bad guys." That was one of the reasons he knew Janae didn't hate him. That she would be good for him. Because even when she didn't need to, she protected him and his memory for Nicole.

"Hmph," he heard his father grumble.

"At least there's that. I'd hate if she'd been told you didn't want her or were dead or something."

He expected them to have some concerns. Hell, he'd acted like a total jackass, so he couldn't expect much more from them. "The first time she called me her dad, I almost fell over. I can't wait for you guys to meet her."

"What about the mother?" This was from his mom. He knew that would be something she worried about.

"Janae is an amazing mother. When I met her all those years ago, she made me want something more. Gave me a glimpse into what my future would be like with her in my life, and it was everything I ever wanted. Then I got called away. This job... it takes so much from you. People don't return. No matter how hard they try. They want a regular life so much, they think they can force it. And when they do, something usually goes wrong. Being who I am, I decided what was best for us and broke it off without another word. I even had Heath block her efforts to contact me."

"Oh, son. What were you thinking?" His father's voice was low and filled with sadness. Noah could tell his words were finally sinking in.

"I knew about her attempts to reach me and ignored every email, phone call, and letter. She'd even attempted to go through my command, but with how things work, they don't give out any information. They'd only pass along the message that she was trying to reach me. After a year, the outreach stopped. She thought I'd left and stopped all contact because I didn't want to be with her. Janae chose to raise our child on her own. She never told me in writing because she wasn't sure what was going on. If you think I'm stubborn, just wait until you meet Janae. That woman does not put up with any mess. Especially mine." He laughed at the thought. They were meant for each other.

His mom spoke first. "So, all this time you had no idea? How has she been able to support the two of them? Are they okay? Do they need anything? When can we meet them?"

Laughing, he almost felt joy but didn't want to put a label on it just yet. "Soon. I promise. I'm still working to convince her we belong together."

"Son, this is a lot to take in. How're you doing with all this?"

Thinking about the question, he smiled. "I'm good. More than good." And he meant it. Life with him wouldn't be easy. Being a SEAL was everything to him. It was his life. His purpose. But he'd been given a second chance, and he wouldn't waste it. "They're my family, Dad. Janae and Nicole belong to me, and I'm not leaving here without them again. I gave up on us before we had a chance to get started. I'm not doing that again."

"Son, then it's time you claim your family. I want all three of you to come visit us. Soon." He loved his parents and knew they'd waited years for something like this. The request was more of a demand, but he understood. He wasn't the only one who'd missed out on the first four years of Nicole's life.

"And I want pictures," his mother called out. "Today, Noah." She'd probably get them printed at the local store and plaster them all over the walls of his childhood home.

"I plan to bring them home soon. I promise. With everything moving so fast, I wanted to tell you what was happening before time got away from me. My command gave me some time off, so I'm stateside for at least a month. I guess they think I deserve it after everything I've done for my country. For the next few weeks, I'm going to get to know my daughter, make things right with Janae, and figure out next steps."

"I know you'll do the right thing, Son."

"I love you, Noah," his mom's voice was shaky. "I can't wait to see my granddaughter. We'll have to get her a college fund set up. Does she know about us yet?"

After a few more minutes of conversation, Noah ended the call with his parents. He shook his head at the pace his life was changing. The only question was, would he be able to handle it?

CHAPTER 14

Janae

True to his word, Noah arrived exactly one hour after they got off the phone. Janae and Nicole decided to wait for him, rather than getting dressed for church. As soon as he arrived, they sat at the table and ate the breakfast he'd brought with him.

This was something Janae never thought would happen. Both she and Noah sitting at the table with their daughter eating breakfast on a Sunday morning. Looking at her daughter's response to Noah, she teared up at all the things her child had missed. Her father being there for her at night when she was sick or cradling her in his arms when she was a small child.

Looking over at Noah's face as he watched their daughter, she knew he'd missed just as much. The look in his eyes as he talked to their little girl, was nothing less than awe. He laughed at every joke, was amazed by her every accomplishment, and he celebrated the little things even she had grown accustomed to as part of their daily life.

Even though she'd been hurt by his departure, it was her own cowardice that prevented her from doing more to find him. She knew how the military worked. If she really wanted to find Noah, she could have.

Shaking her head, she knew some blame for their situation lay on her shoulders. It didn't matter what Heath and Stephanie told her, she could have called his Command and said the magic words. All she'd needed to do was tell them about the baby. They would have contacted him and forced him to get in touch with her. It wasn't that she was looking for money or child support. Those things were important, but they weren't the reason she'd kept their baby. It wasn't the reason she wanted Noah in Nicole's life.

She knew the joy of having a father around as she grew up. Her own heartbreak prevented her from allowing her daughter to have the same thing. That wasn't fair to Nicole. Or Noah. Shame filled her as she thought about what she'd done.

There was a selfish part of her that didn't want him around. Didn't want him to see how broken she'd become after he'd left. Another part of her wanted to prove to the world she didn't need a man supporting her. She would raise her daughter on her own without the need for a husband, or without the stereotype of a man supporting her. She'd been able to do it on her own for years, even in the face of ridicule and hypocrisy. Even her father, the one person she believed would always stand behind her, had disappointed her with his response to her pregnancy.

As the three of them walked up to the front door of her childhood church, butterflies took flight in her stomach. Not in a good way. It was a nauseous feeling. Janae had to force herself to continue moving forward when everything in her screamed for her to run away. To ignore the elephant in the room. The fight or flight instinct rushed through her body, and more than anything, she wanted to choose flight.

As her gaze turned to Noah holding Nicole in his arms, she smiled. Her two favorite people in the world laughed and talked as they strolled up the walkway, and she knew there would be no running away. Not today. Not ever. She'd faced this challenge on her own for too damn long to turn tail now.

Noah would see exactly what she'd gone through. The side glances. The judgment. The innuendo. It wasn't as bad as it was when she was waddling around town with a large belly and no wedding ring, but it was still there. Just under the surface.

Then again, since he was here with her, maybe they'd keep their opinions to themselves. Maybe they would back off for one day. Leave the three of them alone and let them enjoy church services. Laughing to herself, she knew that hope was far-fetched. These people didn't know how to leave well enough alone.

They questioned everything and judged everyone. If anyone didn't live up to the expectations they'd been shackled with, everyone seemed to have an opinion as to what went wrong. It tore at her soul and self-esteem every day for years. They called her a white man's whore, bed wench, Jezebel, and any other name they could think of, to describe how they felt about her sleeping someone other than who they deemed appropriate.

This building, this place of worship, wasn't a safe space for Janae. It was a constant reminder of her numerous failings. Of how she'd lived life on her own terms and had the nerve to not apologize for it. Old ladies told her they'd pray for her soul. Young women held their men a little tighter when in her vicinity. As if she wanted their no-good ass men. Hell, Noah put every single one of them to shame, and once they got a load of him, they'd realize it too.

Seeing her mother standing outside of the church doors, Janae paused. Her legs were frozen in place, and she couldn't go any further. Her breathing began to speed up and her palms started to sweat. She'd forgotten the other part of today's excursion. Her parents would finally meet Noah, the father of her child, the person she avoided naming for all these years.

"Janae? You okay?" Noah's brow dipped in confusion as he looked between Janae and the older woman standing in front of them. Nicole sat in his arms as the two of them stared at her with the same expression of concern.

Janae knew she was acting weird. Freaking out when they had no understanding of what was happening. She tilted her head in the direction of her mother, just as her mother turned in their direction. Janae took a deep breath, alerting Noah that something was about to happen. Stepping closer to her, he rubbed one large hand down her arm. Voice low, he leaned his head down to speak, "Sweetheart, what's wrong?"

Janae couldn't respond. The words wouldn't come out of her mouth. She wanted to turn around and return to Noah's truck. She didn't want to do this. Now that people would know exactly who Noah was, she could only imagine the vitriol that would spew from their mouths. All the women in the church who constantly looked at her with disdain would use this to validate all the hateful things they said about her. She wasn't ready for this. Her mind wasn't ready. Her heart wasn't ready. Glancing at Noah, she knew exactly why she hadn't told her parents who he was.

And her cowardice was about to be put on full display.

"Janae?" Her mother called out to them when she saw them standing there on the sidewalk. "What are you doing just standing over there? Are you okay?" Her mother glanced over at Noah, giving him a curious glance before she turned her gaze to Nicole resting comfortably in his arms. Her eyes swung back and forth from Nicole to Noah to Janae, and back again. Her eyes widened with sudden clarity, and Janae knew her mother had figured it out.

Janae watched in horror as Noah extended his hand towards her mother. "Good morning, ma'am. I'm Noah Braddock. It's nice to meet you." Noah's hand was extended for a few extra—uncomfortable—seconds until Janae's mother finally reached out and grabbed it with her smaller one.

"It's nice to meet you as well, Noah. How do you know my daughter and granddaughter?" As they released their handshake, Noah's gaze shifted between Janae and her mother with one eyebrow raised in question.

Janae closed her eyes, mortified. She knew Noah, even if she tried to deny their connection. There was no way in hell he wouldn't tell the truth. He was proud to be Nicole's father, and she had no doubt he'd tell the whole world if he could. Wild horses couldn't stop this moment from happening. Her breathing continued to come out at a rapid pace, and she wanted to hide. But she couldn't. That option was off the table. Although she'd come to realize the huge role she played in this debacle, there was nothing she could do but watch the train wreck happen.

"I knew Janae from a while back when I was here on temporary duty." Noah was about to continue when Nicole interjected herself into the conversation.

"He's my daddy," she exclaimed. Wrapping her tiny arms around Noah's neck, she pulled her body closer to his while she smiled at her shocked grandmother.

Others heard Nicole's outburst and turned in their direction. Janae looked at Noah and her daughter and noticed the two of them smiling at each other. Her heart squeezed at the vision they made. Another part of her knew this was probably the best moment they would have all day. Glancing back at her mother, she saw the shocked expression on her face morph into a look of anger, frustration, and disappointment.

"Momma. Before you start, just let me explain."

"Janae Marie Hayward," she hissed. "I cannot believe you right now. You could have called to give us a heads up. Is this your idea of a joke?"

Janae stood frozen as she watched her father come out from around the back of the church. He must have been alerted to Janae's presence with a tall white man. His gaze homed in on that same white man holding Nicole in his arms. Her father quickly walked over to them, a frown on his face, as he tried to intercept the conversation.

As soon as he arrived where they were standing, he whispered harshly to his wife. "Beverly, this is not the place for this. Do you want our daughter's business all over this church front yard? This is something we need to talk about when we go home after service. I will not have this family the topic of gossip. Again."

Janae's mother shot him a surprised glare as he spoke. Her hand motioned towards Noah as if to proclaim, *Do you see what is happening*? Janae's father shook his head without saying another word and tried to muster a smile on his face. He looked at Noah.

"Hello, young man. I'm not sure if this is the welcome you were expecting. But as you know, Sunday is a day for forgiveness and peace. Let's focus on reconciliation and time with the good Lord, our father. Whatever else is happening here or going on with you and Janae and my granddaughter, now is not the time for us to address it." Glancing at his wife, he sent her a hard look. "We have a church service starting in a few minutes. We need to get ourselves inside and make sure everyone is seated. After we finish up today, I invite you back to our home with Janae and Nicole. Maybe we can all sit down and figure out what's happening and where we go from here."

Janae hadn't spoken a word besides trying to address her mother when they'd first arrived. Turning her eyes to Noah, she saw his face was tensed in anger. His brow was furrowed, and his lips pursed tight. She didn't know if he was upset with her for not defending him and their relationship, or if he was upset at the reaction from Janae's mother upon seeing him standing by Janae's side.

Either way, she knew she hadn't handled the situation the way she should have. She'd clammed up like a child being disciplined. Behaved as if she couldn't stand up for herself or the man standing next to her. She'd allowed her mother to basically disrespect her and Noah in front of his face. She knew Noah would never turn his anger upon her mother. That's not the type of man he was. As she watched her father pull her mother away and enter the church, Janae turned towards Noah.

"Noah. It's not what you think. Let me explain."

The fire in Noah's eyes made her clamp her lips shut. There was no getting away from this. "You never even told them my name?"

Hurt was reflected in his eyes. She almost reached out to touch him but stopped when he adjusted Nicole in his arms.

"I didn't know how to tell them." Which was a true statement. How do you explain to your parents that you had a boyfriend for over six months and never bothered to tell them about him? A man who came to visit you on the weekends only and left you without a backward glance or a goodbye. The words to tell them she just so happened to be pregnant and he doesn't know because he didn't care enough to pick up a phone or read an email never came out. How would she explain something like that to them? The fact was, she couldn't. She'd been too afraid. Too embarrassed. And when people begin calling her names, white man's whore, bed wench, and so many more, it had all become too much.

"Not good enough. You sat there frozen, while your mother looked at me as if I was dirt on the bottom of her shoe. You let me walk into this situation with my daughter in my arms and allowed your mother to treat me as if I didn't belong here. That tells me more about you than it does about her."

Wetness filled Janae's eyes and trailed a path down her cheeks. She realized the truth of his words. In a matter of seconds, being in her parents' presence had reverted her to a child. What was wrong with her? She wanted him to treat her as his partner. Like a woman who could stand on her own. Someone who could handle the harshness of his world. Yet, she'd just shown him the opposite. "I'm sorry," was all she could manage to whisper, and she knew her words would never be enough.

Parishioners walked by the three of them standing there on the sidewalk. The odd looks thrown their way gave away their silent thoughts. They knew something was going on. The whispers reached her ears as people began to question out loud who Noah was. She was positive word had already begun to travel that he was Nicole's father. Here she stood again, on the outside. This wasn't right. This wasn't how the day was supposed to go. Something inside her knew something would go wrong when they arrived at church. As soon as Noah said he wanted to attend services with them, she knew this would be the inevitable result.

Janae had a choice to make.

Was she going to stand up to the judgmental people in her family church? Or would she turn tail, run away, and hide? Was she ashamed of Noah? No. That wasn't it all. But she'd grown up in this town. Heard all the horror stories about slavery, segregation, Jim Crow laws, and the lingering racism that still existed in North Carolina.

Some in the community have never forgotten the civil rights battles that took place in their state. The *Greensboro Sit-Ins* at the Woolworth's counter in 1960. Or the prosecution of the *Wilmington Ten*, their trial, and the belief they'd been set up by local police and prosecutors. People in North Carolina had long memories, and some were still living in the past. Things were changing but not fast enough.

She didn't live her life for others and tried to never let prejudices drive her. When she'd met Noah, his skin color hadn't mattered one bit. Even though she knew it would matter to those closest to her, she hadn't cared about anything else but being with him. All she'd seen was a man she'd wanted to spend more time with, get to know better, and eventually, they fell in love. Or at least she fell in love.

Janae knew if she didn't face this today, there would be more questions waiting for her tomorrow. Glancing at Noah, she knew he would do whatever she wanted. She also knew Noah wanted to confront this head-on.

"What are we doing, Janae? Are going forward or turning around?" Noah stood in front of her, their daughter in his arms, waiting for her to choose.

That was the question of the day. Wasn't it? Could she move forward and continue to live life on her terms, or would she crumble under the pressure? If she couldn't stand up for her and Noah with her family and their community, maybe she didn't deserve him after all. In the past, she'd been ashamed of what people thought of her and Nicole. She now knew it was because of her own issues. Growing up in a strict Southern Baptist family, life had been about following the Bible, repentance, and doing right in the eyes of God.

Her time with Noah was the first time she'd done something other than what was expected of her. Being with him felt like home. He made her feel loved. Time was no longer on her side. She needed to decide how she was going to live her life from this point forward. Although she told Noah they should slow down, it wasn't what her heart wanted. If anything, she wanted to go full steam ahead. Denying what they meant to each other didn't feel right to her soul.

What they felt for each other and the love they'd shared had created a tiny little miracle, one who was sitting in her father's arms, smiling at them. Looking at Noah,

Janae moved to stand in front of him. She didn't want any confusion about the words she was going to say.

"I'm sorry, Noah. There's more to this than I can explain right now." Shaking her head, she looked off to the side for a moment. "My parents and I have a complicated relationship."

He sighed deeply before reaching out a hand to caress her jawline. "Sweetheart, you don't have to explain anything else. You know I've never cared about the color of your skin, Janae. All I cared about was how I felt when I was with you and how good we were together. I never want you to think I left because I found you lacking or I didn't want to share who we were with the world. That was never the case. You were everything to me, and it scared the hell outta me. Loving each other was never our issue."

Wetness lingered in her eyes as she listened to his words. She wanted to turn around and take her family away from here. Not because she was afraid, but because she didn't want this moment ruined by what she expected to be a hellacious afternoon.

Noah nodded his head toward the doors, "We're here now. The three of us are going to walk in that church together."

Janae's knees were shaking. Walking inside with Noah by her side would send a message to everyone in the church. She no longer cared what they thought about her. She'd almost forgotten that this was her life to live, not theirs. And if living her life to the fullest meant being with Noah, then that's what she would do.

Noah reached out his hand to Janae. "Baby, we can do this. Are you ready to go inside?"

She smiled before placing her smaller hand inside his. "Yes, it's time to face the jury."

CHAPTER 15
Noah

Noah was livid. His hands were shaking due to the depths of his anger at what was happening right in front of him. Janae sat next to him stiff as a board, hands clenched in her lap, eyes straight ahead as she stared at the pulpit. Noah almost got up and left with Nicole several times. This was the most ridiculous situation he'd ever found himself in.

That these people would claim to be Christians was a joke. Noah curled his lip in disgust as he caught the sly glances from some of the congregation, and the pointed one from the preacher. The preacher stood in front of the full congregation and preached Luke 15: 11-32, the well-known parable about the prodigal son. The irony of today's topic was not lost on him. Yeah, he was getting his daughter the fuck out of this backward ass town.

It always amazed him how people judged others by the color of their skin. Especially in the name of religion or their God. This was the church Janae had grown up in. These people had known her since she was a small child. Yet they sat here judging her simply because she chose to be with someone who wasn't black. The preacher's voice caught his attention.

"The son said to him, 'Father, I have sinned against heaven and against you. I am no longer worthy to be called your son.' Can I get an Amen?"

"Amen," a chorus of voices sung out.

He continued, "As I look around today, I see many who have been on this road. Who left the homes of loving mothers and fathers, and turned away from their teachings, and the teachings of the church. Who felt your way of life was better than what you'd been taught. The right way to live. The right way to worship." A crescendo of voices yelled out amen and hallelujah as the preacher wiped his brow. "Some of y'all don't wanna hear me though. You're still out there living life as you please. Thumbing your nose at your parents' teachings. Forgotten the long road we've traveled to get where we are..."

Noah tuned out his words at that point. He knew the preacher was focusing some of his words towards Janae. *Fucking hypocrite.* Janae was not a dark-skinned woman. Neither was her mother nor her father. He smiled at the hypocrisy displayed by so many sitting around them. About half of the church looked as if they were the product of some type of interracial pairing. There were even Latino and Asian parishioners at the church. Yet Janae's mother and father, who was also a Bishop, wore looks of shame and embarrassment. As if Janae had betrayed them, the church, and her entire race.

The longer he sat there, the more he understood why Janae hadn't said anything to them about who he was. Glancing to his left, he saw the woman Sharon, the one who'd been at the ballet class with them yesterday. The smirk on her face was telling. She knew exactly what was happening. She'd probably started sharing the news of Noah's presence yesterday, getting people riled up. Making them question everything Janae said to them in the past. Leaning towards Janae, Noah whispered, "How much longer do we need to stay? I'm ready to storm that pulpit."

Janae's eyes met his, and the look of despair reflected in her hazel gaze made him want to rip this place apart. That she felt so unwelcome in a place of worship was not something he would have expected. This was her family, the people who should love her no matter what. That he'd caused this change to happen with her family ate at him. He never expected the situation to be this difficult.

"Baby, we don't have to stay here." Noah didn't follow anyone's rules unless he chose to do so. Especially when he was out of uniform. His father and mother had raised him to respect people no matter who they were or what color their skin. He wasn't one of those people who proclaimed they didn't see color. He wasn't blind, of course, he did. To him, it just didn't matter.

"We should stay until the end," Janae whispered. "It would look bad if we left in the middle of the sermon."

"I don't care how it looks," Noah growled. "All I care about is getting away from these people." A few turned in their direction, but he ignored them.

"Please, Noah. I've already embarrassed us enough."

He glanced in her parent's direction and shook his head. Her father sat on the dais, behind the preacher. Her mother sat in the front row, next to preacher's wife. Both of their faces were sullen, and he had to hold back a laugh. Parents should never behave this way. It shouldn't matter who Nicole's father was, as long as he treated her and Janae well. What they should be focused on is his return. Whatever this bullshit was that was happening around his women was about to stop.

"Janae, you have five minutes to get up from this pew and go back out to my truck or else I'm going to leave you here."

At the shocked look on her face, he turned away from her. There was only so much he was willing to put up with; slights he would allow to pass. He'd officially surpassed his limit about fifteen minutes ago.

That she was willing to sit here and allow these people to judge her—to judge him and their child—made him question the type of person she was. And that's the last thing he wanted to do. Everything he'd known about her from the first day they'd met up until now had shown him that she was strong, independent, and a good person. He now knew her to be a good mother, an even better woman, and an amazing lover. But how she was behaving today, made him wonder just what the fuck was going on in her head. Had his departure changed her so much?

They should try and keep this out of sight from Nicole. With everything happening around them, there was no way she wasn't impacted by the stares, whispers, and even the tension between Noah and Janae. Noah continued looking at his watch counting down the five-minute deadline he'd given Janae as the preacher droned on about neglectful children.

He rolled his eyes as the preacher seemed to look directly at Janae. The thoughts running through his head weren't acceptable within the church. If that man looked over at them one more time, Noah wouldn't be responsible for his actions.

One-minute to go.

Once the five minutes were up, Noah knew it was time for them to leave. There would be no more of this situation. His daughter was no longer going to listen to this, and neither was he. Janae had a choice, she could leave with him and their daughter, or she could remain in this place and allow these people to make her feel less of a person. If this were the kind of place she intended to bring her daughter to for Sunday worship, Noah would have something to say about that.

Standing from the pew, he tapped Janae on the arm, "Time to get up. We're leaving." He didn't bother to whisper. They didn't deserve his respect. Then again, since everyone had been paying special attention to them, anything they said was picked up by those around them. Everyone turned to look at Noah and Janae. Even the preacher paused in his sermon. Janae hesitated as she looked at the faces staring at them. "Your five minutes are up. I'm not sitting here another second longer. You can leave with Nicole and me, or you can stay here. Make your choice."

Voices began to rise as the ripple effect of his words traveled through the room. From the corner of his eye, he saw her mother coming down the side of the aisle closest to the window, her face scrunched in anger. Shaking his head at this entire fucked up situation, Noah knew he wasn't in the mood for this type of conversation. The day had started off so well, and he had every reason to believe it would stay that way. This was bullshit, and he wanted his family out of here right now. Noah wasn't trying to make a scene, but he was leaving out of this church, and no one was going to stop him.

"Janae, you are embarrassing us. Stop making a scene. Everyone is looking at you."

Of course, Noah thought. Her mother *would* focus on the embarrassment to her and Janae's father, rather than how people in the church kept staring and whispering about her daughter. Aren't parents supposed to protect their children? Aren't parents supposed to defend their children? He didn't know what the hell was going on, but he didn't like it, nor was he going to stick around for more.

"You have three seconds to get up, walk out of this church, and go to my truck. We are not staying."

Janae took one look at his face and hopped up from the pew. Gathering her purse, she looked at her mother and mouthed an apology before she walked toward the front door. Noah followed behind, their daughter held in his arms, with her head resting on his shoulder.

Once they got to his truck, he buckled Nicole into her booster seat. Starting the truck, he turned on the air, rolling down his window for access. He then went around to the passenger side of the truck and walked up to Janae. His arms came up to rest on either side her head as she stood against the closed passenger door.

His gaze took in the woman before him. He wanted to forget and forgive everything that happened just minutes before. Noah looked around the yard of the church. He noticed the green grass, big, tall, old trees, and the old, but well-kept building that should be a symbol of acceptance and forgiveness. From his point of view, all he saw was a place stuck in the old ways of thinking. A place that made those who should be welcome feel like they were outsiders. That they didn't belong if they couldn't conform to a certain way of thinking.

As a child, his parents had taken him to church every Sunday. He attended bible study every Wednesday night. Nowhere in the teachings of any bible owned by him or his parents did he read that those who made mistakes, or those who were a different color than him should not be accepted into the House of God. This place, with its false welcome, and hidden biases, made him disappointed with everything this church stood for.

He'd been in places where religion had caused people to kill women, children, and old men. Experienced the ravages of war all because someone believed their God was the only God that mattered. The results were always catastrophic. Now he was home, only to find out the woman he loved had grown up in a place that made him question why the hell they were fighting in a foreign country. Maybe they needed to focus on their own country first. This wasn't what life was supposed to be about. This wasn't the world that he was trying to build for himself and his children. Looking down at Janae, he knew his face held a look of sadness and disappointment.

"Baby, we couldn't stay in there a minute longer. Did you hear what they were saying?"

Her mutinous look told him she wasn't happy he'd forced her hand and made her leave the church. He knew he'd allowed his temper to get the best of him, but at this point, he didn't care. It was his job to make sure his family was protected, even if that protection was from those they'd known all their life.

"How could you? In front of all my friends and family, Noah? You made me look like a fool."

The hurt on her face almost made him buckle. Almost. Her anger was directed at the wrong person. It wasn't him who'd shamed her. It was those so-called family and friends she still clung to even after everything they'd done to her.

"Janae, I think you need to rethink that statement. I wasn't the one who did this to you or made you feel this way. Did you hear anything said by that preacher today? Did you see the looks from the people staring at us as we simply sat there quietly? The looks of disgust and disdain on the faces of your so-called friends and family? This wasn't something I did. This was something they did to *us*."

Shocked at the direction of this conversation, Noah pushed back from Janae. Running his large hand over his short hair, he thought about if he was ready to fight this battle. He'd only shown back up in her life three days ago. He was already imposing his own sense of responsibility onto his small family. Just a thought in his head brought him up short.

Were they his family?

Did Janae think of him the same way he thought of her? If she had any inkling of how he felt about her, she'd know he'd never stand for them to be treated poorly. Didn't she understand him at all? He'd never allow her or Nicole to be in a situation where people demeaned them, harassed them, or made them feel as if they didn't belong? He loved them. Loved them both more than he loved himself and that truth was tearing him apart.

She didn't understand how much he wanted to go off in the House of God. Even to him, that type of visceral response scared him. The levels he would go to in order to protect them was something he'd only done in times of war. Looking over his shoulder at Janae, he knew the situation between them wasn't going to be easily resolved. They were still expected at her parents' house for a late lunch today. When that was finished, they'd go back to her house and hash this out. Taking a deep breath, he turned back around to face Janae, "Are we still going to your parents' house?"

"I don't know if you'd even be welcome at this point." Rolling her eyes, she opened the passenger door of the truck and hopped inside. Noah knew he was in the doghouse from what he'd done. He knew it. Understood it. Didn't mean he would have changed a damn thing.

If he was going to be in her life, both she and her parents needed to understand how things were going to be from this point forward. No one, and he meant no one, would make Janae feel that way again.

CHAPTER 16
Janae

Janae wanted to go home. Not to her parents' house but to her own home, where she could feel comfortable.

Church services would be over in a short while, and her parents would be headed back to their home. She knew they fully expected to see Janae and Nicole waiting for them. Whether or not they wanted to see Noah there with her, she didn't know. She didn't want to face the situation if she didn't have to, but that was taking the coward's way out. Sitting in Noah's truck as they drove to her parents' house, she wanted to tell him to turn around because this was never going to work.

The way he'd acted in church today wasn't something she would get over. Who cared if the preacher was doing a sermon that seemed to cut into her with every word he spoke? It didn't matter that the women in church stared at her with a mixture of disgust and outrage. No one could judge her. They'd already tried and failed to stop her from living her life. Their approval was not needed. But Noah's behavior was outside of the norm, and he'd made a spectacle of them. Taking a deep breath, she tried to calm her nerves.

She could admit that he wasn't the only one who'd been out of line. She'd done that all on her own with her silence, secrecy, and multiple lies by omission.

They were both giving each other the silent treatment. Noah was angry. She was angry. Nicole probably felt the tension between the two of them, because even she was quiet throughout the entire ride.

Today was going to be the day everything was made right. They would get their lives back on track and become a family. Within minutes of arriving at the church, everything had turned upside down.

Why couldn't her parents just accept the situation for what it was? Janae was not a child. Her parents sometimes behaved like she was, and to her fault, she allowed them to do so. She was the mother of an impressionable young child. Someone dependent on her to show them the way. To be strong. Brave. Bold. It was time her parents understood that. Looking out the window, she watched as the scenery flew past them. She loved this place, and her life Jacksonville. But maybe it was time to make a new beginning someplace else. Maybe this was no longer the best place for her or her daughter.

"Janae, I'm not going to apologize for what happened. If I had to do it all over again, I would."

Janae laughed silently to herself. She knew, if given a choice, he'd do exactly what he'd threatened. It was something about the way he handled situations. If someone was out of line or stepped to him the wrong way, Noah took care of the situation swiftly. From their brief time together, she vividly remembered that personality trait. They'd gotten into it a couple of times because of it. She didn't feel every situation required a reaction. Noah disagreed.

She should have known exactly what his response would be when they walked into that church. Few white people came to New Bethel Ministries, and if they did, they only came once. She'd always thought of the church as a welcoming place. That the congregation would open their arms to anyone of any race, creed, or color. United by the only thing that mattered—their love of God.

As she thought about it, she knew that wasn't the case. They were old-fashioned in their ways. Maybe insulated was a better word. They didn't welcome strangers into their world without taking them through the wringer first. It was an old church. It had been built from the ground up by a former slave family. For better or worse, memories in her community were long, and not always fair or forgiving.

Glancing at Noah, she knew he'd done the right thing by making her leave. Even if she didn't want to accept it at the time. No one had ever gotten up in the middle of the Pastor's fire and brimstone sermons. He probably gave that man a heart attack.

"I know, Noah. You did what you thought was right. I can't judge you for that."

Nodding his head, he glanced at her before turning back to the road. "Then why are you still upset?"

"Because I wasn't ready for the changes that are about to happen." Thinking about the confrontation that was about to take place with her parents, her stomach almost turned over. She knew this day was coming, she just never thought it would be here so soon. Her parents were a force to be reckoned with. Then again, so was Noah. In this situation, she'd rather have him by her side.

"Do you want to go to your parents' house? If not, I can turn around."

Noah was giving her an out, which she was tempted to accept. But this was something she could no longer avoid. "No, let's keep going. We need to have this talk with them. I don't know what's going to happen with you and me in the future, but they need to know the truth. They'll need to know you're going to be in their granddaughter's life from now on. I won't allow them to say negative things about you in front of Nicole when she talks about her father."

Noah's hands tightened on the steering wheel. "Listen, I don't know your parents, and after today I'm not sure if I really want to. But I will tell you this, if they attempt to say anything negative about me, or anything to do our family, I will not allow Nicole to be around them."

"You would try to keep my daughter from my parents?" After saying the words, she admitted she never thought it would be a possibility. Maybe having Noah back in her life wasn't such a good thing after all. He couldn't just make everything his way or the highway.

"You're damn skippy I would. If your parents do anything to turn my child against me now that I've just found her, I will bring the wrath of the entire Navy upon your parents to make sure they never see her again."

Janae had no words. She knew her parents could be extra. She knew they held strong opinions about interracial marriage, especially when one of the people was African-American. They believed in black love. But their belief in black love blinded them to other kinds of love. If you were gay, don't show that behavior in their church. If you loved someone outside of your ethnic background, keep it to yourself and don't go out in public. Her parents were old school, and she could appreciate that to some degree. But many of the beliefs they held onto were hurtful. Their way of thinking made people feel unaccepted and alone.

Thinking about Noah's words, she knew he had a point. Her parents could be quite horrible at times, and it could be difficult to get them to see reason. On the other hand, she wouldn't allow Noah to run roughshod over her life. That they were still her parents. She would simply have to handle them the best way she knew how. Make them understand how things were going to be from this point forward.

"So, what happens when this doesn't work out? When you return to Virginia and I'm the one still stuck here in this town? You'll no longer be here to protect us now that you've made a grand statement. At some point you're going to leave, right? And I'm going to be by myself, surrounded by people with long memories. Then what?"

Silence filled the cab of his truck. A small smile came over his face, and he lifted one eyebrow in that sexy way of his. She knew that look. He was up to something, and she wasn't sure if she'd like it.

"Sweetheart, I never said I was leaving North Carolina without you. This may be the perfect time to do it. I need you to understand something, Janae. From the moment I found out about Nicole and realized you still loved me, I had every intention of bringing you back to Virginia with me. Before we leave North Carolina, I'm going to make you my wife.

"What?" she yelled, scaring Nicole awake.

"Mommy?"

Turning her head to look in the backseat, she smiled at her little girl. "Sorry, baby. Mommy didn't mean to yell so loud. Everything's okay."

"You sure, Mommy?" Turning to Noah, her little asked him the same question, "Daddy, is Mommy okay?"

Every time she called him by that title, Noah's smile got bigger. Janae rolled her eyes.

"Yes, Nicole, your momma's fine. It's okay. Lay back down. We'll be at your grandparents' house in a few minutes."

Janae was fidgeting in her seat as she wanted for her daughter to settle down again. Turning up the music playing on the kid's music station, she turned to Noah. "I don't know what you're playing at, but I'm not having it." Her voice was tight with tension. She didn't like to be toyed with, and that's exactly what it felt like Noah was doing.

Noah glanced at her with a determined look on his face. "I'm not playing at anything. I'm telling you what I plan to do. My track record may not be so good with you, but that'll change. Did you think I was joking when I told you I came back to claim my family?"

"Well, yeah! I kinda did. You know how military men spout off shit all the time. Why would I believe you want me now when you didn't want me back then?"

She knew her words were petty. He'd told her, several times, what his reasoning was back then. She'd claimed to accept his explanation, but there was still something inside her that doubted him. A little devil on her shoulder who whispered in her ear, telling her he was only saying the words he thought she wanted to hear. They probably gave classes to military men on how to handle breaking it off with the women they left broken-hearted. With extra credit classes on what to do if she ended up with your child, and you found out years later.

She could see his jaw clenching, as if he were grinding his teeth. "I'm not going to discuss this right now. There are small ears in the truck, and I don't want her to hear us arguing. You're fighting me on this simply because you think you should. Not because you want to."

Crossing her arms, she wanted to deny his words, but knew she couldn't. "You don't know what you're talking about."

Nodding, he glanced at her with a hard look. "I do, and you know it. Now, put a smile on your face. GPS says we're pulling up to your parents' house. And if the car speeding in my rearview mirror is anything to go by, I'd say your parents are right behind us."

CHAPTER 17
Janae

Janae looked at Noah in shock. "Explain yourself please. What do you mean you want to marry me?"

"Not sure how else to say it. I had every intention of marrying you before I left to go back to Virginia." Noah had a look on his face as if daring her to challenge the words coming out of his mouth.

Janae looked in the side mirror, watching her parents as they stepped out of their own vehicle and walked up to the house. She knew today's events had thrown them for a loop. Just showing up with Noah in tow was a surprise, but it was the only way she'd have the nerve to introduce them.

From the moment he'd walked back into her life, she knew she was no longer willing to let him go again. If that meant her family life would be in upheaval, she was willing to take the risk. Closing her eyes for a second, she thought about everything they'd gone through in the last few years. They'd been through hell and back, even if they hadn't been together during that time.

Even though her parents didn't like that she had a child out of wedlock, they'd supported her. Her father, for all his grouchiness and outdated beliefs, had never wavered in his love of Nicole. She was his granddaughter, his princess. It just so happened that the way she came to be was less than ideal.

Noah turned to her as they sat in the driveway. "Babe, you have to suck this up. I'm not hiding away. I'm here now. And you need to face your parents, because they need to know what the deal is." He paused for a second as he gazed into her eyes. "What exactly did you tell them about me, us, our relationship?"

Janae didn't know how to answer his question. She'd kept so many secrets from everyone over the years, the truth had started to blur. She didn't want anyone to look at her differently, so she'd shut them out to protect herself. It didn't do any good though, because they'd treated her differently anyway.

"I didn't tell them anything. It was something I kept to myself. I didn't want all the questions coming my way or the assumptions about things unsaid. If you haven't noticed, people are nosey around here. They make it a contest to see who can find out the most information about someone. Mainly gossip and rumors. I didn't want them asking where you were or why you weren't with me. It would have been too much. At the time, I was already dealing with so much."

Janae felt tears welling in her eyes, and she tried to fight them back. She didn't want to cry in front of him. In a matter of three days, he'd come back into her life and turned everything sideways. For so long, she thought she'd never have this chance to talk with him again. To finally understand why he chose to stay away. She'd dreamed of this moment for so long, but words failed her. Turning her head away from him, she looked at her childhood home. Her mother stood at the front door, arms crossed across her chest, and one foot tapping as she stared at the vehicle with Noah and Janae inside.

"It's time for us to go inside. I can't hide you forever, even though I wish I could."

Janae laughed a little at her own joke. If she had her wish, she would have Noah locked away in her house where no one could take him away from her. Where even the military couldn't get to him, asking him to put his life on the line again for a country, or people, who didn't want him there.

He motioned to the backseat, "I'll grab little miss sleepyhead. You go on up and meet your mother. We'll be right behind you."

Stepping out of the truck and walking up to the front porch, Janae had to remember that her parents meeting Noah was a good thing. She knew her parents had also suffered from her situation. People questioned what type of parents they were, to raise a daughter who would have a child out of wedlock with a military man who had only been in town for a short time. As long-term members in their church, they were considered pillars of the community. They'd had to defend themselves against those who questioned their ability to serve their congregation.

Even through everything, and even though they were unhappy with her decisions, she knew they loved her. However, her mother's earlier reaction to Noah wasn't something she understood. Her mother wasn't racist—even if she had some skewed views about how people should live But her behavior with Noah before church made Janae question what she knew of her mother and her views on race relations.

Even now, as she watched her mother stand impatiently on the front porch, Janae didn't know who this woman was. This wasn't the woman who raised her. Then again, maybe it was, and Janae had simply never known who her mother truly was. Looking over at Noah as he and Nicole walked to the front porch, Janae knew this was her moment of truth. It was time for her to break free of her mother's shadow. Her entire existence had been focused on trying to do the right thing and trying to be the best daughter her parents could have. She now realized that by trying to be the perfect child for them, she'd forgotten how to be herself.

All the years she'd tried to force herself to be the type of person her parents, their neighbors, and the church members expected her to be, had finally taken its toll. Glancing at Noah again as he picked up their daughter, she realized holding on to her parents' ideas of who she was supposed to be, was going to make her miss out on her future.

As she reached the bottom steps, her mother gave her a disdainful glare, raking her eyes from the bottom of Janae's shoes to the top of her head. What she found was clearly lacking in her eyes, and it almost made Janae burst into tears. She held back the feeling of hurt coursing through her veins because she knew she'd done nothing to deserve this. Her father, on the other hand, seemed to be more accepting of the situation, if only he'd been the one to greet them at the door. At this point, Janae had enough of kowtowing and begging forgiveness. Was her decision to be with Noah going to be the thing that tore them apart? She couldn't believe how hateful her mother was being but it no longer mattered. Either she accepted that Janae would make her own decisions, or she wouldn't. That wasn't Janae's problem anymore.

"Are you sure you want to do this?" Noah asked in a low voice.

Nodding her head, Janae knew there was no backing out of this situation. This confrontation was long overdue. She was positive her parents were going to question why she'd kept Noah a secret for so long. She'd have to stay strong for this meeting and not become weak again in front of Noah.

How could she demand he stand up for her and Nicole to the entire world, when she couldn't even do it with her parents?

"I'm as ready as I'm ever going to be," she smiled over at him. Stepping over the threshold of her childhood home, she strolled inside with her head held high, Noah and Nicole right behind her. Her father came down the hallway, with a huge smile on his face as he always did.

"Hey, sweetheart. You finally made it inside. For a minute there, I thought you were gonna make a break for it." Her father opened his arms as he continued walking toward her, and Janae knew that was his way of expressing his support. Her parents had been married a long time, and it was usually her father who had to step in to smooth over ruffled feathers. He seemed to be in that mode again.

"Hey, Daddy," she drifted into his arms, accepting the comfort only he could give. This was the man who taught her how to ride a bike, how to pray, and who always had her back when she needed it. Even when she'd done things she knew would test his anger.

"It's going to be okay," her father whispered. "She just needs more time."

Pulling back, Janae looked at her father with an expression of disbelief. "More time for what?"

Her father's eyes glanced up towards Noah and Nicole standing by the door speaking quietly to each other. "I guess we just didn't know what to expect. While I may seem calm on the outside, I do have a lot of questions. Your mother, on the other hand, is a little more... vocal about her concerns. Baby, you just never told us anything about the man who was Nicole's father. You have to grant us a moment of shock. I mean, this is a bit of a surprise."

"I get that, Daddy. I really do. But momma's response to Noah was out of line. She didn't have to treat him that way. She looked at him as if he was scum on the street. You guys know nothing about him, and that was intentional on my part. Noah was my secret to keep, and mine to tell. Because of the situation, I chose not to tell you anything. But it doesn't mean he is any less of a man deserving of respect." She knew she was pushing her luck. She'd never actually spoken to her father this way before. It wasn't that she was disrespectful, but she was firm in how she expressed herself. They'd raised her to be a strong, independent woman, not some weak doormat. She only hoped their teachings didn't backfire on her today.

"Well, we're about to learn all about him today. Aren't we?" Squeezing her arms with his large hands. Her father gave her a loving look as a smile hovered on his lips. They both knew today would be interesting, but Janae was positive she was up for the fight. "I know this is your life, Janae. Your momma and I have tried to stay out of it. Even when you came to our front door with a belly full of baby, no ring on your finger, and lips clenched tight whenever we asked about the father. All we ever wanted was the best for you, which is all any parent wants for their child. Life can be difficult for a single mother of a mixed-race child. It was never our intention to make you feel as if you couldn't tell us the full situation."

Tears welled in her eyes as she listened to her father speak. Biting her lips, she nodded to let him know she heard and understood his words. She knew the way they grew up was different than the world today. A single black girl becoming pregnant by an absentee white man was not something accepted by families or the community in their time. For it to happen to their own daughter, must've been jarring to them.

Now, Noah had returned. Waltzing into their lives as if nothing had happened, or at the very least, everything could be made right. She knew how this entire situation looked to her parents and felt a twinge of guilt for not giving them more time to prepare. Giving her dad a wobbly smile, she whispered, "I know, Daddy. I promise we'll try to explain as much as we can."

Nodding down at her, her father smiled at the scene across the room. "We'd better get over there. The two of them look like they're about to get into some trouble."

Looking over her shoulder, Janae noticed Noah and Nicole, whispering to each other, gesturing wildly. It looked like they were plotting something. "I think you're right."

Turning away from her father, Janae walked over to Noah and Nicole, "Nicole, say hi to your granddaddy."

"Hi, Papaw," her little girl sang out, giving the old man a hug around his waist.

"Hey there, baby girl. You being good for your momma?"

"I sure am. Papaw, my Daddy came back from fighting the bad guys." Nicole beamed up at her daddy, her face lit up with happiness and hero-worship.

Janae's father looked between Noah and Janae with a confused look. "I see that."

Janae figured now was a good time to step in. "Lieutenant Commander Noah Braddock, US Navy, this is my father, Bishop Lawrence Hayward. I figured it was best if you two had an official introduction."

Noah stood to his full height, reaching out his hand to her father. "It's nice to finally meet you, sir."

"It's nice to meet you as well, Lieutenant Commander."

Noah shook his head. "Sir, please call me Noah. I only use my title when working."

Her father gave him a shrewd look, "And what exactly do you do for the Navy?"

Noah looked at Janae at the same time she turned her eyes to him. They hadn't discussed what they'd tell her parents about his job. She shrugged her shoulders, it was up to him what he shared. Since she hadn't told them anything about him, the ball was in his court.

Turning back to her father, he smiled. "As my daughter said, I fight the bad guys."

Just then, Janae's mother stormed back into the foyer. "If we're going to have this discussion, then let's do it now. I don't want to spend my entire day talking about something that's only going to upset me."

Looking over at Noah, Janae noticed his raised eyebrows as a look of frustration covered his face. She saw his eyes glance down at Nicole, and she knew exactly what he was trying to get across to her. He wasn't going to allow their daughter to listen to Janae's mother saying anything negative about him or Janae in front of Nicole. Sighing, she knew this day was probably about to get much, much worse, because honestly, she agreed with him.

She'd thought this would be a wonderful experience for Noah to meet her parents. To understand the people and place she'd come from. Give him insight into the person she was and make him realize that coming back to them was the right thing to do. Maybe she'd been wrong.

Pasting a smile on her face, she looked at her mother, "Momma, I love you. But I'm here today to introduce you and Daddy to Noah, Nicole's father. I want this to be a good day for all of us. A day where we come together as a family. I need you to do this for Nicole and me. But if you can't, we'll leave, and this meeting will never take place. It would be too bad if that happened, but I won't subject Noah or Nicole to negative comments."

Her mother went to open her mouth to say something, but her father placed his hand on her arm and shook his head. "No, Bev. I think we need to listen to our daughter. We need to understand her side, and Noah's. They're both here today, with our granddaughter, standing in our home trying to make this right. I won't have us making our own daughter, or her guest, feel uncomfortable. So whatever issues you have going on right now, I'm gonna need you to hold them inside. I'm hungry. I want to spend time with my granddaughter, and then I want to watch the football game. Can you give me that?"

Janae could see her mother fighting against her father's words, even though her lips were still held tight. Her mother was a fighter. Had been her entire life. If she felt answers were needed, she would go after them like a dog with a bone. And Janae knew, even though she wanted to deny it, this situation demanded answers.

After a few seconds, her mother sighed and nodded her head. "Okay, Lawrence, you get your day." Turning back to Janae and Noah, she gave them both a half-smile. "Lunch is in the dining room. Go on in and seat yourself. Nicole, come with Grandma, so we can wash your hands."

Everyone in the room gave a collective sigh as Janae's mother seemed to accept that she wasn't going to get the fight she'd been itching for. At least not today. Janae knew if her mother couldn't hold her tongue, Noah would have picked up Nicole and simply walked out, just like he'd done at church. Glancing back at him as they followed her father into the other room, she didn't know how to express how happy she was that Noah had returned to her. Not only had he given

Nicole what she'd been missing for so long, but he was also giving her back the voice she thought she'd lost.

As she smiled at the thought of her family coming together, her heart stuttered. What was that old saying, *A fish and a bird can love each other but where would they live?*

CHAPTER 18

Noah

Three hours later, they were leaving Janae's parents' house. Nicole was knocked out, and Noah was holding her in his arms as they exited the front door. For the most part, he was pleased with how everything had gone. The first hour had been tough but nothing he couldn't handle. Janae's mother was no pushover, but he could respect that.

Reaching out his hand to Janae's father to say goodbye, he thought about the man he'd gotten to know this afternoon. He was a good man. A godly man. A man who loved his daughter. Someone who only wanted the best for their child. A man just like his own father. He hoped someday he would become the type of father others looked up to and wanted to emulate. Raising a daughter was not going to be easy, he knew there would be challenges; no matter what, he was ready to face them head-on.

"It was good to meet you, Noah. I hope we get to see a lot more of you. Maybe the next time you stop by, we can take the boat out and do some fishing."

"That would be great, Sir. I think I'd enjoy that." As Janae was giving her father hug goodbye, Noah turned to Janae's mother, holding his hand out to her as well. "It was nice to meet you, Ma'am."

"Well, I'm pleased I got to meet you as well. Who knew you would come back into our lives in such a way?" Her gaze slid to Janae as she spoke. Shrugging her shoulders, she splayed her hands in front of her in a gesture of surrender. "If my daughter's happy, then we'll accept her decision, and from the look in your eyes, I doubt my daughter stands a chance." She smirked at him, as if she knew something he didn't.

"Ma'am, I plan to make your daughter my wife. I know it. She knows it. Now I just need to make her accept it." Adjusting his daughter in his arms, he looked over his shoulder at their vehicle. "We'd better get on our way, Janae. It was nice meeting you folks. I'm sure we'll be seeing each other again soon." Noah turned away and began walking towards the car, giving Janae a few more minutes with her parents to say their goodbyes.

Once he'd settled Nicole into her booster seat, he climbed behind the wheel of his truck. His thoughts went to the woman walking towards their vehicle. He knew he had a lot of work ahead of him. Being married to someone in his profession wasn't going to be easy. There would be long days and nervous nights as he was away on missions. He'd tried to save her from the heartache when he'd walked away the first time. Shaking his head derisively, he laughed as he thought about how well that plan had worked out for him.

Walking away from Janae just wasn't going to happen. She made him feel. She'd made him want more. When he'd left back then, he truly thought it had been the best thing. But something was missing from his life.

Janae.

It had always been her.

He was ashamed to think about some of the things he'd done while they were apart. If he could scrape those memories out of his brain, he would do it in a heartbeat. He didn't know what Janae's life had been like while they'd been separated, but if their experiences at the ballet studio and church were anything to go by, she'd taken the brunt of the issues, pain, and hurt that came with having his child. For that alone, Janae deserved everything he could give her and more.

Janae opened the door, climbed inside, and gave a huge sigh of relief. "Well, that went better than I thought."

Laughing, Noah shook his head. "You think so, huh?" Starting the truck, Noah put the vehicle in reverse and backed out of the long driveway. They waved to her parents as they stood on the front porch watching them leave. "Is everything okay? Your parents both had smiles on their faces when you came to the truck. Did things get settled?"

"As much as they can be. They may not be completely happy with the situation, but at least they understand now. They know you never knew about Nicole. They understand it wasn't intentional that you stayed away while I went through my pregnancy and raising our daughter alone."

Noah still couldn't believe they'd gotten to this point. He was glad Heath had called him about Janae. If Stephanie hadn't come clean, Noah would still be in the dark. "You know we'll need to visit Heath and Stephanie soon, right?"

Nodding her head, Janae looked over at him with an uncertain look on her face. "Yes, I know. Although, I'm a little worried about what he thinks of me now. Not only did I keep this secret from you, but I pressured his wife to keep everything secret from him. I know I did it for reasons I thought were best, but I don't want there to be long-term issues. I know how close the two of you are."

Reaching over, Noah grabbed her hand within his. Squeezing it tight, he gave her a small smile as he continued driving. After a few seconds of silence, Noah spoke. "Heath is my brother, so we'll always be okay. Once he found out about Nicole, I would expect nothing less of him. Stephanie... She's like a sister to me, and I know her loyalty was torn between keeping your secret and telling her husband. I'm actually surprised she kept this from Heath for so long."

Noah also knew he needed to tell Janae about his family in Virginia. It was an unorthodox family consisting of a hodgepodge group of people who'd come together over the years. Some were still in the military, and some had finished their time and hung up their uniforms for good. Others joined the family by default, mainly through marriage. But his family in Virginia, those were the people—outside of Heath—that he'd give his life for. Now that he had Janae and Nicole, it was time to bring the two of them into the fold.

"I've lived in Virginia for quite a few years now," he opened. "While there, I've met people I consider my closest friends, my family."

"Family?" Janae's voice was low and questioning.

Glancing at her, he saw a look of worry on her face. He knew what was going on in her head. Did that family in Virginia include a woman he'd become close to? Someone who wouldn't be happy once the news of Janae and Nicole got out? He almost smiled at the frown marring her brow. As if there could be anyone in his life who could mean as much to him as she did?

He continued speaking, ignoring the thoughts he could almost see swirling around in her brain. "I think everyone will love you. There are four other guys who I'd call my brothers. We basically adopted a woman named Adele after she relocated to Virginia. So, there are six of us." Navigating the roads, taking them back to her home, Noah thought about the steps he needed to take to move Janae and Nicole to Virginia.

"A couple years ago, Adele went and got herself married to a Jarhead name Stefano, and I have a precocious niece named Sophia who's somehow managed to manipulate every single one of us. Not sure how that happened, but I'm sure Adele's husband had something to do with it. Next, Ethan found someone who could put up with him and married a wonderful woman named Vanessa, and has an amazing stepson named Damian and new little boy he named after me. Tyler, another Marine, will be retiring soon, and he recently got married as well."

"Wow, so you guys just came together out of the blue?" A smile hovered on her lips.

"Sort of. A few of the guys do the same work as I do, and we met either on base or on missions. The others I met at a boxing gym we all go to back in Virginia."

"So, I don't understand. You're stationed in Norfolk, but you met some of these people in Alexandria. How does that work?"

Noah was pleased Janae was attempting to get to know more about him by asking questions rather than making accusations. He knew mentioning Adele's name would prompt questions about who she was and what she meant to Noah. It was odd for him to mention a female's name in front of her, even in their time together before. While he knew her curiosity about Adele was probably burning a hole inside her brain, he was glad she was giving him more room and time to discuss the people in his circle.

"As you know, Norfolk is a small town on the eastern shore of Virginia. Although our base is there, it's not necessarily a place where I want to settle down. When I retire, I'll need to be in a place where I can put my skills to work. Northern Virginia is that place. Adele's husband approached me and the others about working with his security company once we retire."

Shaking her head, Janae just smiled at him. "You already have a job when you retire?" At his nod, she went silent, staring at him with those gorgeous light brown eyes of hers. "Tell me more about Adele. How did she and her husband meet? What kind of security company does he own?"

Noah would need to be careful with how much he shared about Adele and her background. Even when she explained everything to him and the other guys, it had been difficult for him to accept. "Adele relocated to Virginia a while back. When the guys met her at Hank's gym, they knew she would fit in with our group. She was looking for a change in her life and wanted to start over. Her husband, Stefano, is a guy who did his time in the Marine Corps. When he got out, he decided to put his skills to use in the civilian world while also making a ton of money from a lot of rich people."

"So, Adele is just some woman you met and decided to claim as your sister?"

Shaking his head at the simplicity of her statement, Noah smiled to himself. While that was the basic truth of who Adele was, she'd become so much more to not only him, but the other guys as well. She was their sister, no matter what. Meeting Adele opened their eyes. Helped five battle-hardened men see they didn't have to close themselves off from the world all the time. That life was about more than fighting the next fight or going out on the next mission. "I wouldn't say she's just a woman we *met*. Adele was someone all five of us gravitated toward because she needed us. *Not* in the way you might be thinking. Adele moved to Virginia to fight her own demons. In the process, she met my brothers and me, and later, the love of her life."

Just as they arrived at Janae's house, Noah's phone rang. Pulling it out from the center compartment of the truck, he looked at the number and saw it was Tyler calling. "Do you mind if I answer this? It's Tyler from back home."

"No, I don't mind." Janae went to get out of the car. But Noah stopped her as she put her hand on the door latch.

"It's okay, Sweetheart. Stay. Wait for me to help you get Nicole into the house. This shouldn't take long."

Swiping the screen, he placed the phone at his ear. "Noah, here. What's up, man?"

"Hey. Where are you? We've been going by your house, and you haven't been home. Ethan says you're not answering his calls.

What the fuck, man? You disappeared on us."

Noah could hear the frustration in Tyler's voice, which was unlike his friend. "Brother, why do you have stress in your voice? What's going on?"

"Adele and Stefano want us to come by their house on Saturday. After Adele couldn't get in contact with you, Stefano even tried to call. Now, you know if he's trying to get in touch with you, Adele must be freaking out. So, where are you? Can you make it to Adele's house?"

Noah looked over at Janae, sitting in the truck next to him. He knew she could hear Tyler's voice coming through the phone, but at no time had she given any hint that she was disturbed by what she heard. He knew what he wanted to say, what he wanted to do, but he wasn't sure Janae was ready for that just yet. "I'm out of town right now. I'll call Adele and that stupid husband of hers later today. But yeah, I'll be there. Any idea what this is about?"

Tyler's laughter came through the phone, "I'm not telling you. You know Adele likes to keep her secrets, and this is one I fully agree with. If it's gonna get your ass back here to Virginia, then I'm keeping my big mouth shut. Plus, you know Adele. She's always trying to pull the family together to build memories. She says it brings us closer or some soft shit like that. The woman swears it'll give us good things to hold on to when you guys go off to play shoot 'em up bang-bang."

Smiling at Tyler's words, Noah thought of how bossy Adele could be with five guys more than twice her size. Even with everything she'd gone through, she never let them forget she was just as tough as they were. "Yeah, that's Adele. All right, man, I'll be there."

"A'ight man, I'll see you there. I'll tell Adele and Monica the good news. So, are you finally gonna tell us where you've disappeared to this weekend?"

"What's Monica got to do with this? What are they up to?"

Tyler's uneasy chuckle came through the phone. "Nope. Whatever's going on, I'm leaving it up to those two. My name's Bennett, and I ain't in it. You just get your ass to Virginia. Now stop changing the damn subject. Where the fuck are you, man? You never go off on your own like this. Keep it up, and I'll have Daniel come find you. Make him force you to give up the goods."

A shiver went through Noah at the threat. There was no way he wanted Daniel digging into what he was doing. He needed more time to prepare Janae for a life with him. The time to introduce her to his family would come soon enough. He just had to make sure his new family was ready for the chaos they were about to get pulled into. It had only been a few days since he'd come back into her world, and he now realized his demand to know why she wasn't prancing him out in the streets had been answered several times over. This shit was more complicated than going on a SEAL mission on two-days' notice with only half of his team.

"Stop being so damn nosey. Mind your business, Jarhead." Noah hung up the phone to Tyler's laughing. If he didn't love that dude like a brother, they'd probably be at each other's throats. Tyler was a ball buster and never failed to get in someone's face, exactly at the worst moment possible.

"So, which one was that?" Janae began unbuckling her seatbelt to exit the truck.

"Tyler."

"And... who is Adele again?" Noah again heard the uncertainty in her voice as she opened the door to exit.

Climbing out of the truck from his side, he walked around to where Janae was standing on the other side. Wrapping his arms around her waist, he pulled her tightly to his body. "Baby, you never have to worry about Adele. She is my sister. Nothing else. There is no one in this world she loves more, or who loves her more, then her husband. Well, let me change that. She loves her brothers more than life itself, but Stefano is the man she fell *in love* with. Now you... You're the only woman to ever hold my heart. Always have been, even when you thought I'd forgotten about you."

Her eyes seemed sad as she looked up at him. "I heard you say something about you would be there, at some type of event. Are you leaving? If you have to go away for a bit, it's okay. It's *okay*, Noah, I'm not going to be *that* woman."

"What does that mean?" Noah smiled at her, because he knew exactly what she was talking about. He'd seen plenty of those women in Norfolk. The ones who constantly whined and pouted when their men had to go on missions. They could never seem to wrap their minds around the reality that their boyfriend or husband had a job to do. He knew going back to Adele's get together at her house wasn't anything associated with the military, but he still appreciated Janae's wording.

"It means, we just came back together. You had a life before this. Before Nicole. It means I'm not going to give you shit because something is going on back in Virginia that your friends and family want you to attend." Lifting her chin, her eyes met his, "And it means, if you want to do something for work or for your family, I'm not going to be the one to hold you back. But I also won't be the one sitting here waiting and pining for you if you choose not to return."

Shaking his head, Noah knew she meant every word. He was the one who'd come back into her life, not the other way around. He was the one who'd barged into her world, demanding his place by her side. It was a small thing, going back to Virginia next weekend. But it also raised other questions.

When he left, would life go back to normal for him? Would he forget about everything that happened this weekend? The answer came swiftly. Absolutely not. He'd made his choice. He was going to be with this woman, no matter what.

There was no way she was getting away from him a second time. Noah was committed to building a life with Janae, the way he should have all those years ago. And that beautiful little girl sitting in the back seat of his truck was never going to know another day without him in her life. He was always going to be her father, regardless of whether he was on a mission, stationed in another city, or anything else that attempted to pull him away from his family.

"I will always come back for you, Janae. These years we've been apart no longer matter. You are my home. Nicole is my home. And no matter how many times I leave for work, I will always come back to you."

CHAPTER 19

Janae

Noah was back home with them, and Janae's heart was full again. Him being away from her and Nicole for more than a week had been too damn long for her peace of mind. When he'd returned from attending the event his sister had at her house the other weekend, Noah had been in an especially good mood. Turned out, Tyler's wife Monica was pregnant. Noah was excited about being an uncle again, talking nonstop about the things he would do with the child once born.

As they lay in her bed, she looked over at the man who made her dream of things she wasn't sure she wanted. When he'd left her, she thought her world was over. Jacksonville was a little town trying to pretend it was big. Although the Marine Corps base was situated near their town, many of the people who grew up there still behaved as if their little town was the center of the world. That's one of the reasons it was so difficult for her to be on her own. Everyone expected all the locals to act a certain way. Allowing someone in the military to get you pregnant, knowing they could leave at any moment, was never viewed positively.

Trailing her finger down his bare, tattooed chest, she smiled at the sight in front of her. Noah was a good man, and he treated her like a queen. What woman wouldn't want a man like him by her side? As they'd continued talking about what happened during the time they were separated; she'd come to know him differently than before. Back then, it was the excitement, the mind-blowing sex, and all the ways he could please her. And she him.

As they got to know each other all over again, she realized there was so much more to Noah than she'd first thought. Her fingers continued tiptoeing down his body as he lay naked underneath the covers. Not only had he come home to her, but he'd made sure she knew just how much he'd missed her.

Nicole had been in bed, dozing off to sleep the night he'd returned, but Noah made a point to go to her room to let her know he was back. Their daughter had been asking about him the entire time he was away in Virginia. True to his word, Noah called them every single night to catch up on their day. Even if it was a ten-minute conversation to tell them how much he missed and loved them both.

She knew Nicole had been missing him something fierce. In her eyes, her dad had just come back into her life, only to leave again. Janae was savvier this time and didn't react with panic and negativity. Because of his work, and the life he had in Virginia, it would take time for them to find their rhythm. North Carolina was just a hop, skip, and jump from where he lived, and for the time being, they would make this work for them.

Even though she knew Noah was probably tired from his travels, and their exertions once they made it to the bedroom, she wanted more. Janae began to kiss Noah's bare chest, moving her soft lips over his hard body as he slept away. It wouldn't take much to wake him, so she continued her quiet seduction. Sliding her hand down his body, she pushed the covers away from his waist, looking at the thick appendage lying to the left, resting on the inside of his bare thigh. Licking her lips, she moaned low under her breath as she relived their activities from last night.

Even at rest, his cock was something to admire. Such a simple thing gave her so much pleasure. Then again, it was more than likely the man it was attached to. Adjusting her own body, she slid her leg over Noah until she was situated on top of him. Her pussy still wet from their earlier session, she began to slide her slick channel up and down his thick cock. Leaning over Noah, she whispered in his ear, "Noah, wake up. I want you."

Within a matter of seconds, Noah's eyes flew open, almost jarring Janae as she sat on top of him.

"Hey, Baby." He moaned in a sleep-filled voice. "You want more?"

"I always want more. I've missed you."

"I missed you more, Baby." Noah's hands reached up from the side of the bed and grabbed her firm ass. He squeezed his hands along her soft skin as she began rotating her hips, sliding her already wet pussy over his awakening cock. They both began to moan from the sensual feeling of being connected again.

" I know it's only been a week, but I'm glad you're back. I was beginning to go through withdrawal."

"Is that right?"

"Yup," she answered.

"Look at you..." he whispered huskily. "So damn beautiful..."

Her head was spinning as he lay back on the bed, intense green eyes staring at her naked form. She could feel his desire for her in every delicious, agonizing grind of their hips. His grip tightened on her body as he slid his cock along her wet slit. Noah grimaced, as if in pain from forcing himself to go at her pace and not take over. Smoothing her long fingers and painted nails across his rippled, ink-covered chest and down to the dark pubic hair of his crotch, she gazed at him, enjoying this moment.

A wicked grin came over his face before he spun them around. He was now leaning over her as she lay back on the pillows. Janae relaxed on the mattress and stared up at him, a loving smile on her lips. Finally, he looked at her, and when he did, her eyes filled with tears.

"Make love to me, Janae. Claim your man."

Janae's heart melted. "Yes. You belong to me, Noah," she whimpered. Noah leaned down, bringing his lips to hers. As they kissed, he wrapped around her and rolled over, setting her on top of him again. She leaned over, bringing one of her bare breasts closer to his mouth. He lifted his head, clasping his lips around the nipple. Noah closed his eyes tightly as he suckled her flesh. She reached down between his legs and stroked his cock until he was gasping for breath.

Janae sat up, separating her breast from his mouth. She pushed her lower body down, pressing her hot channel against his thickness. Sliding down, she impaled herself with his cock, and her mouth opened in ecstasy. Even after making love to him all night, his size still filled her to the brim, stretching her wide, and going deep inside her body.

She watched Noah grit his teeth as she impaled herself on his hard shaft. His breath came out in harsh pants as she rolled her hips on top of him. Green eyes focused on her with increasing intensity. Raising his knees, he gave her something to lean back on. She moaned loudly as she tried to hold back her orgasm. Hips pumping, hands grasping her hips, he held her tight as they made love in the early morning light. The feeling coursing through her body caused her mind to short-circuit.

Pleasure pulses triggered in her brain. Her stomach fluttered and her toes curled. She continued grinding on him, her hands bracing her upright over his chest. She kept her eyes closed because just the sight of him would make her come, and she wanted this to last. Janae couldn't hold back the gasp of ecstasy. The minute the sound released from her; her body was overcome with sensation. Her orgasm would not be denied. Opening her eyes, she looked down at him. A keening whine traveled up her throat as her body locked up. Wetness flowed from her body to coat his hard cock as he fucked her harder and harder.

Noah sat up and grabbed her body within his embrace. His arms wrapped around her back, cupping her shoulders within his hands. He continued pumping up into her body. His motions prolonged her orgasm as tears began to fall from her eyes. She wanted to escape the overwhelming sensation, and at the same time, never wanted it to stop.

His jaw clenched and his eyes shut tight. As he continued his onslaught, masculine grunts escaped from deep in his throat, sending her into a chorus of moans. When she collapsed on top of him, she took a moment to catch her breath. Pressed against him this way, she felt a light coating of perspiration wherever their skin connected. As his grip tightened around her back, he whispered in her ear. "I love you, Janae. I love you so much. Thank you for giving me a second chance."

She sat back to look down at his face. Smiling down at him, Janae took note of his expression. Concerned. Determined. Focused. He was afraid she'd reject him.

"I love you, too, Noah Braddock."

At those comforting words, tears ran down the sides of his face. He held her tight against him, like he'd never let her go. When his hips lifted and his thick cock penetrated her again, they both gasped with pleasure.

"You feel so good. So fucking incredible," he breathed, as he stroked inside her. His hands grasping at her smooth skin, squeezing the soft flesh of her breasts. She dug her nails into his hard, muscled chest and groaned in pleasure. It was slow. It was deliberate. Noah was making sure it was just how she liked it. Slow. Deep. Hard.

Loving the damp heat between her legs, she clenched her teeth and tried to hold back her orgasm. She wanted him to come with her. To her delight, she watched his chest rise and fall from exertion as she began to spin into an explosive climax. She arched her back and closed her eyes tight, holding on to the feeling. Janae felt her body burst with pleasure as he pushed all the way in, pumping deep and hard.

"Damn. Baby. Take all this dick. Fuck, Janae. Your pussy feels so good."

Noah pumped harder and faster as they both chased their release. An erotic death swirled into a kaleidoscope of pleasure and pain. She gasped, and her eyes opened to look at his face. His green eyes were glazed over with lust and desire.

Grinning at her, he licked his lips before hissing. "Yes. That's it, Baby. Give it to me."

He thrust inside her deeply, groaning loudly as she used her nails to scratch at his skin. Janae could barely hold on as her body went along for the ride like a cowgirl taming a bucking bronco. A waterfall sensation came over her entire body in a flash of fire. Grunting like an animal, she pressed her hips against his as hard as she could and felt his cock throb inside her.

Noah closed his eyes and grit his teeth as he came. His entire body shuddering with chills as his fingers gripped her hips with enough force to leave a mark on her skin tomorrow. Still catching her breath, she gave him a wicked smile as she watched him.

"You look fantastic when you come," she whispered sensually.

"Only with you, Sweetheart." Lifting his upper body, he grabbed her close, capturing her lips with his in a wet kiss.

Once they broke apart, she connected her gaze to his. "You are the only man I've ever made love to like this before. You take care of me so good, Noah."

Rubbing one hand down her chest, he palmed each breast as he bit his lip. "I'm addicted to you."

"I'm addicted to you more." He ran a finger down her body, reaching the spot where her hip met her groin, and she burst out laughing. He remembered how ticklish she was in that spot. Falling over his chest, she wiggled her hips before wrapping her arms around his chest. "God, I'm glad you're home. I don't want lose you again."

They lay together in silence, letting the significance of her words sink in. They both knew the Navy forced him away in the past, and they'd do it again and again until he retired his commission. Nothing in this life was promised. A new assignment or mission could come any day, and he'd have no choice but to leave. They were both keenly aware that he'd have no other option but to go where they needed him, heading off into danger to save the world. It didn't matter that he'd requested time off to spend with her and Nicole. If the Navy beckoned, he would have to go. Just the thought of that put a damper on the entire morning.

Noah lifted her body from his, setting her to the side on top of the mattress. Swinging his legs to the other side, he sat frozen for a moment before taking a deep breath. Janae knew he was thinking about all the "what if" scenarios. She'd done that so many times over the years, she could probably give him a few new ones to think about.

Just as he moved to lift from the bed and clean up, she grabbed onto his arm and stopped him. "Nothing is going to happen to us, Noah. I promise you." Now if only she could believe her own words and stop the feeling of impending doom filling her.

CHAPTER 20
Noah

"Janae. We need to talk about you meeting the family." Another month passed with Noah down in North Carolina. The more time passed, the more certain he became that the call would soon come and he'd have to leave. Not that he wasn't trained and prepared for whatever came his way, but leaving Janae behind without a connection to his life in Virginia wasn't okay with him.

Eyes wide, she paused in the act of making breakfast for the three of them. "So soon? I mean, we just found each other again. You're still getting used to being a father. We're still getting our footing with our relationship. No. I don't think that's a good idea."

Noah watched as Janae paced around the kitchen. Nicole was putting together a puzzle in the living room, so her attention was elsewhere. Good, because he and Janae needed time to hash this out. Something was wrong with his woman, and he needed to figure out what was going on in that head of hers. "Sweetheart, what are you worried about? Why don't you want to meet everyone?" He noticed she was biting her nails, which was a nervous tic she's had for years. "Janae. Talk to me."

She took a deep breath, her gaze avoiding his. "What if they don't accept us? I don't know those people, Noah. I refuse to put my baby in a situation where she's not welcome. What are they going to think about you bringing your black baby momma to meet them? Child in tow and begging for acceptance. Nope, I won't do that to my child."

Holding in his temper at the slight, Noah's turn was harsh. "She's my daughter, too. Do you think I'd ever place her in a situation where she'd be harmed or hurt in any way? Haven't I proven anything to you these past months? I love Nicole. As a result, my family will love her." He ran a hand over his hair, his frustration evident in that rough motion. "Janae, stop acting like this. I want her to meet my family."

"Those people aren't your family," she spat at him. Janae's face was screwed up in anger.

Noah was shocked at her outburst. He had no idea where this was coming from. "Janae, what the fuck? Why do you have a problem with the people I call family?" Noah's mind whirled with questions.

She began hyperventilating as wetness fell from her eyes. "None of them even knew about us before now. What exactly have you told them about me?"

Noah didn't want to have this conversation. Nothing he could say would make things better. If he told her the truth, she'd never forgive him. All her fears would be validated, at least in her head. But he also refused to lie to her again. "They don't know about you and Nicole. That's why I want the two of you to come with me to Virginia. This isn't a conversation to be had on the phone. The entire group needs to be there to meet the two of you. I'm going to have a lot of explaining to do, so I'd rather do it in person."

Taking a deep breath, she looked at him with a question in her eyes. "Why do you owe these people so much? You didn't feel you owed me anything for years."

At her question, Noah stood from his chair. His hands flew to his head, rubbing along the short hair. He thought they were done with this. They'd gotten through so much these past weeks. Her parents, the gossip about their relationship, and building a future together. No, it wasn't what he'd envisioned for himself when growing up, but this was the one in front of him. Yet, they were still only living a half-life, with part of him still connected to Virginia in ways he couldn't explain to her satisfaction. On the other hand, what he was building with Janae and Nicole was as real to him as anything else. He wasn't going to let her push him away like this.

"Why did you say they aren't my family? After everything I've told you about them and what we've gone through. Why would you say something like that?" Noah ended his question in a near yell. He was trying to keep things quiet with Nicole in the house, but it wasn't working.

"Mommy? Daddy?" Nicole called out to them from the living room. He could hear her little feet skipping along the carpet. He moved to go to her, but Janae stopped him.

"I got this," she muttered.

"This conversation isn't over," he hissed.

Looking at him over her shoulder, her face was sad. "It is for now. We can talk later tonight."

Noah didn't like the tone of her words. Nor was he going to allow her to hide behind their daughter. If she had a problem with his life or the people he chose to be around, then she needed to be honest with him. Not throw little fucking temper tantrums. Especially not when he was trying to merge his two worlds. Watching Janae and Nicole as they sat on the carpet playing with the pieces of a new puzzle, Noah knew his woman needed a bit more convincing. Good thing he was up for the job.

Later that night, Noah was sitting on the edge of the bed when Janae walked into the room. "She asleep?"

Janae paused after closing the bedroom door. "Yes. But I have to tell you, our little girl is smart. She kept asking me if we weren't friends anymore."

Tilting his head to look at her, Noah could admit he had the same question. "I'd like to know what happened as well, Janae. What's going on with you? I've never hidden anything from you. The only things we don't talk about involve my work and what I do for the Navy." Sighing, he rested his elbows on his knees. Briefly closing his eyes, he opened them to look at the woman standing across the room. He felt a wedge coming between them but had no way to fix it. "What's going on, Baby?"

She stood silent, arms crossed in a protective gesture, as they stared at each other. "Noah. I'm scared."

Standing from the bed, he walked over to her. Bending his knees, he positioned his face so he was looking into her eyes. "Why are you afraid? There's nothing to be scared about when it comes to my family. We're in this together and things are going to be just fine. I love you. I love Nicole." Standing up straight, he used one finger to lift her chin. Her light brown eyes glistened in the darkness. "Baby, I need to know you're taken care of. Do you understand what I'm saying?"

At his words, her entire demeanor changed. Janae's face crumbled as tears began flowing from her eyes. Sobs escaped her mouth as she grabbed him around the waist, pulling their bodies close together. All he could do was hold her in his arms as her emotions poured out, wetting his bare chest. Breaking his heart into pieces at the same time.

"Baby, please. What's wrong? Talk to me, Janae."

Her cries tore at him. Noah could barely make out her words when she began speaking. "Don't wanna lose you... Going away... Family... Me and Nicole."

"It's okay. Take your time. Let it all out." Noah shifted his body, grabbing her up in his arms. Walking them to the bed, he lay her down before positioning his body next to hers. That she was fully clothed and he was wearing only his boxers ran through his mind quickly. But since he wasn't a fucking animal, he let the thought fly away into the wind. His woman was hurting something fierce. Based on her words, he now had an idea why. She wasn't angry at him or his family in Virginia. No, this wasn't about them at all. This was about their life together.

Their future. What would happen to her and Nicole if he left one day and didn't come home? Because it was a real possibility. The threat of a bullet to the brain, or a roadside bomb, or any number of things could take him away from her, no matter how much he'd want to return.

"I'm sorry," her soft voice whispered in the silence. The worst of her tears seemed to have stopped.

"Talk to me, Janae. What's going on with you?"

After a few seconds of silence and sniffling, she spoke. "Meeting your family in Virginia makes it real. I know why you want me to meet them, and I'm having trouble with it. You want me to have a support system in case you don't return one day. People who'll be there for Nicole and me if you die. I know what that's all about. I've seen it here and met women who've gone through it."

"Is that why you acted the way you did earlier today when I mentioned going to Virginia?" Noah's brain was playing catch-up. Women were interesting creatures. Damn confusing, too. Maybe he should call Adele to get her opinion on what he should do. This was not his area of expertise, and he had a feeling he was failing miserably. Dealing with female emotions wasn't a skill he was trained on in the Navy. And at thirty-five, he'd never bothered trying to learn.

"I can't lose you, Noah."

Wrapping his arms tighter around her waist, Noah tried to reassure her. "And I don't want to leave you. When I retire, you'll never have to worry about me leaving again. But until then, I need to know you and Nicole are taken care of. I've started the paperwork to have her recognized as my daughter. There are some things I need to finalize in Norfolk, so you both need to go with me. I also want to make sure I have things arranged for you. That means getting you connected with my people in Virginia. I need you to meet Adele and the guys. Their spouses are an extension of them, as are their children."

"How soon do you want to go?"

"As soon as you can get some time off. I'm not asking you to upend your life just yet." He wanted to but knew that would be a bad move.

"What? I'm not ready to move to Virginia," her voice rose volume.

"No, you're not. Not yet, anyway. The day will come when I'll need to return to Virginia full-time. When I do, I want the two of you with me. I'm not willing to be away from the two of you for longer than I need to."

Lifting her head, she turned her body over, so they were facing each other. He wanted to smile at her red-rimmed eyes and swollen nose. Janae may think differently, but to him, she looked beautiful.

"What about my family? My job? You can't expect me to just give up my life here."

He knew this would be the bulk of her argument against moving to Virginia. Lifting one hand, he pushed a few strands of hair away from her face. "You're amazing. You know that, right?"

Smacking his hand, she rolled her eyes, a small smile on her lips. "Stop changing the subject."

"I'm not. Simply stating a fact. No matter what's going on, you are the only woman for me. You're beautiful in every way, even when you wake up in the morning with your eyes full of crusties and drool stains on your chin." Her laughter at his words made him smile.

"I don't drool," she exclaimed with a laugh. "Well, you're the one who snores." She harrumphed, casting her gaze down, her bottom lip pushed out in a pout.

"Sweetness. Hear me when I say this," Noah lifted her chin with his finger. "Too much time has been wasted. My fears and my lack of faith in our relationship kept us apart for too long. Those years could have been spent creating memories with each other, and our daughter. I know it may seem fast to you, but I'm not willing to walk away from you again. I know this would be a sacrifice. Your family is very important to you. But you are important to me. I want us to start our lives together, and I'll do whatever it takes to make that happen."

"I guess I hadn't thought about what the future would hold. It makes sense that we'd live in the same place, of course. Traveling back and forth between Virginia and North Carolina won't make sense long-term. I get it," she paused, taking a deep breath. "What will I do in Norfolk while you're gone?"

"You wouldn't be in Norfolk. You'd be at my home in Fairfax. That's the home I'd retire to, the place where I want us to raise Nicole."

"Fairfax?" Janae became quiet, her face contemplative. "You seem to have this all planned out."

"Not all of it. The important stuff, yes. I need the two of you settled before I leave for my next assignment." He knew this next part wouldn't be easy for her. "My gut's telling me I don't have much longer. The time's coming for me to go away soon. I can feel it. Before I leave US soil, I need to make sure you and Nicole are going to be okay." As she opened her mouth to speak, he placed a finger on her lips. "No. No more fighting me on this. Not now. Not anymore. Baby, I'm serious about you being my wife one day. Hell, I'd rather it happen right this moment, but I know it's not possible. I've never been more certain about anything in my life. I'll give you as much time as I can, but you need to know, you're mine. I'm never letting you go again. You will be my wife one day soon."

Her eyes were wide, the tears long gone. "That was some statement, Lieutenant Commander Braddock."

"You damn well know it." Reaching a hand down to the waistband of her yoga pants, his fingers dipped inside, rubbing against her wet slit. "Now, make love to your man. They say make-up sex is the best kind."

"Mmmm," she moaned. Using her own hands, she pushed her pants down, removing them from her body as he continued playing with her lower lips. "Wait." She pushed back to look him in the eyes. "That was a marriage proposal, right?"

"That was a marriage promise," he said, just before sliding one digit inside her sweet, tight, delicious pussy. "Come here." Rolling her onto her back, he slid one leg between her thighs. "Don't you think Nicole needs a little brother or sister? Because I think it's time we try for a second one." Removing his finger from her wet channel, he coupled it with a second one before sliding them back inside. Fucking her hard with his hand, Noah looked down at the women writhing in his arms. Her moans filled the room, her scent permeated his nostrils. His mouth watered at the smell of her juices. "Oh, baby. I need to taste you." Shifting his body down, he lifted both her legs, placing them over his shoulders. Taking a moment to enjoy the view, he pressed his nose into her mound and inhaled. His cock thickened in response.

"I'm not ready for another baby," she moaned. "Marriage first."

Using the tip of his tongue, he swiped at her hardening clit. "Does that mean you won't make me wait to marry you? I want you as my wife, Janae." He licked her pussy from the bottom to the top. Her moan was loud and guttural. "Want to see you pregnant with my child." Noah sucked her clit into his mouth, sucking the flesh hard, flicking his tongue on the hardened nub. Janae widened her legs. Her hands attempted to grab at him. Although she was speaking, he didn't think it was real words coming from her mouth. The only thing he understood was his name. Releasing her flesh from his mouth, he swiped his tongue along her nether lips. "Come to Virginia."

"Yes!"

Lick. Suck.

"Meet my family," he cajoled.

Suck. Lick.

"Fuck. Noah! Yes. Anything you want."

He inserted a finger into her dripping passage, resulting in a keening moan escaping Janae's lips.

"Marry me. Give me what I need. Don't ever leave me, Baby. I'll never let you go again. You belong to me. Always have."

His fingers continued to drive inside her pulsating channel. Hips lifting from the bed, she began humping his digits, her body careening toward an orgasm. Using his other hand, he removed his boxers. His cock was leaking precum, ready to claim his woman.

Janae's mouth opened in a silent scream, her fingers grabbed the sheets underneath her, and her body tensed. Noah could feel the wetness flowing from her body. Removing his fingers, he positioned his hips between her thighs. Pressing her body down against the mattress, he grabbed his cock, placing it at her clenching slit. Pushing inside, he groaned at the sensation. "So tight. Yeah, that's it, Sweetheart. Take all this cock."

Her eyes opened, a smile came over her lips, and her hands reached up to hold him around the waist. "I'm never letting you go again. You're mine, Noah."

"Damned right, I am," he whispered. Instinct took over from that point. He drove his cock into her body as if nothing else mattered. And to him, at this moment, nothing did.

Noah knew being with her was the right thing for him. He felt complete. He'd been waiting for this moment his entire life. Now all he had to do was get a ring on her finger before the government called him to do their bidding again.

CHAPTER 21
Noah

"Tell me the plan for the week again?"

Noah could hear the nervous tenor of Janae's voice when she spoke. Driving up the interstate always soothed him. The open road, the lull of the music as he allowed his brain a moment to rest. Well, that was how it used to be, before an important little human rode in the backseat of his truck and the woman he loved sat next to him.

Grabbing Janae's hand in his, he placed a soft kiss on her soft skin. Lifting his eyes to look in the rearview mirror, he smiled at Nicole's sleeping form. His heart constricted as he thought about what they were doing. "Baby, stop worrying. We're gonna spend time with the guys and their families, plus Adele and hers. That's it. I want you to relax, be yourself, and give them a chance to get to know you."

Noah focused again on the road ahead of him. He held up a brave front for Janae, but this was the first time in years his stomach clenched with nervous anticipation. Facing the enemy was easy. Admitting to his friends he'd had a child he didn't know about was the kind of shit that made him wince in embarrassment.

"I'm just nervous. After what you went through while staying with me in Jacksonville, I'm almost afraid of what will happen. Will your friends accept Nicole and me? I won't have her treated poorly, Noah."

Shaking his head, he squeezed her hand in his. "Just two more hours. You'll see. Everything will be fine," he promised, a tinge of hope in his voice. Thinking about the confrontation he knew was coming, he wanted to avoid having Janae see any of it. She wouldn't understand what was happening or why his friends were so angry. At least, not at first. He took a deep inhale, focusing his mind on the task at hand.

First, get his family to his home in Fairfax. Second, call Adele to let her know he was back and had some people for her to meet. Third, gather everyone at one spot to introduce Janae and Nicole. One... Two... Three. He wasn't nervous at all. This weekend would be easy as pie.

Hell, even he wasn't crazy enough to believe that bullshit line.

*****

"What the fuck do you mean, you have a child?" Ethan's loud voice carried through the backyard and into the house.

Noah was already at his tipping point. The meeting with Adele and Stefano had been good, after some fast-talking. It took a lot of explaining to get Adele on board. That alone conveyed how important the two people sitting in her home were to Noah. He didn't usually explain himself to anyone. Few people made him want to give anything more than a cursory statement. Adele was one of them. Plus, he needed Janae and Nicole to be accepted into the family. He had a feeling he was working on limited time. His girls needed to be with the family when he left this time.

Ethan's attitude wasn't helping the situation one bit. Noah brought his hard gaze to Ethan, bristling at the anger wafting off the other man. Noah stormed over to Ethan, coming within inches of the other man's face. "Say one more fucking word, and I'll put you on your ass. That's my goddamn daughter in that house. You're my brother, Ethan, and I love you, man. But I will fuck you up if you say one more thing about Janae or Nicole." Tension filled the air as the two men stood toe-to-toe, chests heaving with harsh breaths.

"Enough," a loud yell startled the group of men. Daniel stood off to the side, one leg hitched up on a bench situated around a pond in the backyard. "What the fuck, Ethan? Why are you always the one losing your shit? I expect it from Tyler or even Tony, but I thought you'd calmed that shit down."

"Hey! What'd I do?" Tyler called out.

Tony lifted his beer. "Leave me outta this shit. I haven't said one word, so don't bring me into Ethan's bullshit. Not this time, bro."

After a few moments of silence, Ethan exhaled loudly, and his head fell forward on his shoulders. He took some deep breaths before lifting his head to stare at Noah. Hurt was reflected in his gaze. "You have a daughter. A little girl you've known about for over three months. Yet, today is the first time we're meeting her. We're supposed to be family."

Noah understood more than the others why issues with family impacted Ethan harder than the others. The man still held demons inside from the murder of his sister by her abusive husband. Ethan's wife, Vanessa, had calmed some of the storm raging inside him, but there was still enough inside him to cause moments of concern. It was situations like this, the fear of his family dynamic changing, when Ethan flared, and his emotions became volatile.

Stefano Indellicati stepped up to the small group. As Adele's husband, he was given some leeway with Noah and his brothers, but not much. Ethan and Tony still wanted to get him in the boxing ring and kick his ass. Noah was tempted to give the green light but knew their sister would never forgive them.

"Ethan, if anyone would know better, it would be you. You've known Noah longer than any of us, know him better than any of us could." Stefano tilted his beer toward Noah. "He didn't know about Nicole before six months ago. Now that he does, he's doing the right thing. The first step is introducing Janae and their beautiful little girl in there."

Eyes full of hurt and anger, Ethan glared at the man trying to bring calm to a volatile situation. Even during a Saturday afternoon cookout with family and friends, Stefano looked ready for a magazine shoot. Noah rolled his eyes at the man who was never seen with a hair out of place.

"Whatever, Jarhead," Ethan smirked before stepping back. "She's my niece first. You're just related by marriage."

And there he was. Ethan had gotten over his moment and was back to his normal, ball-busting self.

Daniel jumped in, "So, what's the plan? They here to stay? Is she ready for what this life might bring to her doorstep?"

They all knew the words were intentional. If Noah died in battle after he and Janae were married, she'd get a visit from a military chaplain on her doorstep to tell her the news. Noah hadn't prepared her for that eventuality. Not really. The possibility of him being injured was something they'd talked *ad nauseum*, but not his true death. Could he really deal with the thought of leaving them on their own?

What if he died and left them on their own? His heart twisted in his chest at the thought. Rubbing a hand down his face, Noah sighed. "I need her connected to us. Nicole and Janae mean everything to me now," he stated. "Brothers, it's been too long since I've been pulled out. I feel it coming soon. Last time I left her, she was carrying my child. This time, I need her to know she's not alone." He walked over to the cooler and grabbed another cold beer. "My little girl takes ballet. Can you believe that shit? Wears a pink tutu and ballet slippers. She's pretty good, too." A smile covered his face as he pictured his daughter's smile.

"What the fuck? You going soft on us, Ghost?" Tyler laughed, slapping him on the back."

"Hell, no. Not for the shit that counts." He paused, looking over his shoulder. "You know, when Vanessa and Monica came into our lives, I was happy for you guys," he said, nodding at Ethan and Tyler. "But, honestly, I didn't fully understand." He smiled, "Now I do."

Head nods and smiles were all around. Even from Tony and Daniel, who were both semi-single. Daniel was doing a not-so-secret mating dance with Monica's sister, Charity. Tony was still fighting his attraction to a woman who wanted nothing to do with him, but one who Tony couldn't stay away from. They all knew what it felt like to find the person who made them complete. Noah lost his woman years ago to his own selfishness. He wasn't letting that shit happen again.

Draining his beer, Noah threw the empty bottle in the trash. "I need to check on my girls." He gave a two-finger salute to the guys and walked to the back door, entering Stefano and Adele's home.

"No, Janae. You're not going anywhere. Noah brought you here to meet his family. That means something." Adele and Vanessa stood next to Janae, while Monica leaned against the counter a few feet away from them. The laughter and yells of the children could be heard from the other room.

Noah never expected to be happy to hear a child's laugh. Today, he was, and it was the best fucking sound he'd heard all day. What bothered him was the discussion between the women. Was Janae really trying to leave? "What's going on? Why are you trying to leave?"

Four sets of eyes turned to him but no one spoke. They all knew who the question was spoken to.

"How about we go into the other room?" Vanessa gave a soft pat to Janae's shoulder while giving her a sympathetic look.

"Sure," Adele agreed, before giving Noah a tight smile. "Seems like maybe you two need some time to talk."

"Why do I have to leave? I wanna see what happens," Monica quipped, before popping a pinwheel wrap in her mouth. At the dropped jaws around the room, Monica's eyes went wide as she chewed her food. She shrugged her shoulders and attempted an innocent look. "What? I'm just asking. Damn, y'all never let me have any fun."

"Get your pregnant behind in the living room. Don't make me call Tyler in here." Adele lifted one arm and pointed her finger towards the open space. "Get going wobble-wobble."

"Ugh, I hate it when you guys gang up on me. Hold on, let me grab more food. This baby is like a garbage disposal." Monica grabbed a plate and began loading food on top as the other ladies kept shooing her out of the kitchen.

Noah took everything in with a neutral expression on his face. Their antics would often bring a smile to his face. Not today. Not when he didn't know what the hell was going on and why Janae was trying to leave. They'd just arrived. Once it was only the two of them, he walked over to her. "What was that about?" Janae looked everywhere but at him. Grabbing her chin within his hand, he lifted her face so he could look into her eyes. "Talk to me."

Janae shook her head, a look of frustration on her face. "I told you I wouldn't put my daughter in a situation where she wouldn't be accepted. I told you that!"

"And she's not. Have you heard the laughter coming from the other room? Our little girl is surrounded by people who want her to be happy." Noah knew Janae was feeling out of her element, but she had no reason to. These men would protect her with their lives. Treat her with the same respect they would their own wives.

"Your voices carried from outside. The windows are open. What happened out there? It sounded as if you were about to come to blows. So, explain to me why your friends are so angry? Because if you can't, then Nicole and I are out of here. Your choice."

CHAPTER 22
Noah

"Hey, Adele?"

"Yeah?" the tiny woman responded with a knowing smirk on her face.

"Janae and I are gonna step into the other room for a minute. Can you keep an eye on Nicole?"

Nodding her head at him, she pointed towards a room down the hallway. "Stefano's office is a quiet space. He had it soundproofed. You know, just in case," she smiled.

Noah shook his head at Adele, "Get your mind outta the gutter, woman." He and Janae began walking down the hallway so he could get her in a private space. Doubting his intentions at the beginning was one thing, but he needed them to get past this if they were going to have a future. He couldn't be on foreign soil, focused on his mission, trying his damnedest to come home alive, if Janae was still worried about this kind of shit.

"It's always in the gutter," Adele yelled at their retreating backs.

He turned his head to look at Janae, "Ignore her."

Laughing, she shook her head. "Nope. I like your sister. Hell, I like all the wives. Even Monica, who's kinda mean."

Opening the door to Stefano's office, he led her inside before closing and locking the door behind them. "Monica's not mean." Nicole gave him a look, and he put up his arms in surrender. "Okay, I take that back. She's mean as hell, but she loves Tyler, and she loves being part of this family. Plus, she's pregnant, so we're giving her a pass."

"Yeah, okay, if you say so. This is a nice office." Her eyes took in the space, the family pictures, the military photos, and the dark paneling.

Seeing it through her eyes, it looked like a normal home office for a successful businessman. Well, Stefano didn't do anything normal. Behind the façade of family photos and memorabilia, was a man who did whatever was needed to keep his clients safe, the money flowing, and his business growing. His methods weren't always... clean, but they were effective. Noah knew going into business with Stefano was something he wouldn't pass up. The brothers had discussed it after he and Adele had gotten married. Tony had already paved the way for them, testing the waters so to speak. When Stefano approached them about joining the business as partners, they'd been surprised. Global clients, some in countries they'd visited as part of their military duties, some who lived in palaces with so many servants, they hardly needed to wipe their own asses. If walls could talk, this office would have many tales to tell, including some that were better left secret.

"It is. Stefano likes to be surrounded by only the best." Both in his personal and business life. Noah leaned up against the large desk, folding his arms over his chest. "Janae, we need to get past these issues you're having. We need to get through whatever concerns are still going through your head. I won't have you second-guessing me, or my commitment to you, while I'm gone."

Sighing, she looked up at him, a small frown over her face. "I know." She paused before walking over to him, stopping just inches away from his larger frame.

He didn't move or adjust. If she needed to get something off her chest, this was the time to do it. Life was too short to have all these fears and hang-ups. Hell, his own family had gone through enough shit. Adele's abusive ex-husband coming back to try and kill her. Ethan's sister killed by her abusive ex-husband. Vanessa losing her first husband while he was fighting in another country. The stalker who terrorized Monica for months. Anyone who joined the family had to be all-in. He knew Janae would get there eventually, but something told him he needed to speed up the timeline.

"If I told you it was my completely unjustified anxiety that you were still embarrassed by us? That even though every woman in the other room is a black woman, that your brothers still won't accept us because of the color of our skin? If I shared my irrational concern with you, what would you think?"

Noah's heart stopped. Shaking his head, he looked at Janae with a puzzled look. "I'm confused. You're going to have to explain this to me as if I'm a child. Even though three of my brothers are married to black women, you somehow think they won't accept you and Nicole because you're black?"

The woman had the nerve to look embarrassed. Yeah, she should be. *What the fuck was this crazy shit?* "Why?"

After a few moments, she began pacing in front of him. "When you've been raised a certain way all your life, it's hard for those lessons to disappear. I know it's stupid, and you've never made me feel as if you're ashamed of me. Living in a place saturated with stories of white men and how they treated black women, the lines begin to blur. Old fears return. Stories shared with me as a child, and even as an adult, return to mind when I think about the two of us making a future."

Noah took a deep breath. Rubbing his fingers across his eyes, he wanted to yell, scream, tell Janae to let that stupid shit go. But he knew it would be the wrong thing to say. This wasn't about him. This was about her moving forward and shedding the heavy cloak of bigotry that dogged her for years. "Baby, do you love me?"

"Yes." No hesitation.

"Do you believe I love you?" Janae paused to look at him, opened her mouth to speak, then closed her lips again. Noah stood up straight, unfolding his arms. He stopped her pacing and grabbed her hands within his. "Janae, answer me."

"I believe you want to love me. I believe having Nicole in your life is the most important thing to you right now."

"Baby, you and Nicole both are the most important things in my world. Without you in my arms, nothing else fits."

Sighing, she looked at him with those light brown eyes that did him in every time. "What if this feels right because you're trying to force it? In reality, we've been together one-year, yet we have a four-year-old little girl. Everything is so different. What if Nicole and I move here with you and you fall in love with someone else? Someone who doesn't look like me. Where will Nicole and I be then? Out on the street and out of the family?"

His head was about to explode. Janae was thinking of every reason he wouldn't want her, except for looking at the reasons he did. Closing his eyes, he tried to come up with the right words to say. How could he make her understand what he was feeling right now? Focusing again on Janae, he saw the nervousness she felt reflected in her eyes.

The fear that he'd abandon her again. *He'd done that. His actions were what made her feel this way. It was his fault. Not hers.*

Pulling her into his arms, he leaned against the desk again. It was his turn to share something he never thought would be spoken out loud. Slowly, he began to tell her his truth, expressing feelings and actions he never thought he'd share with her. "These past few years, I lost myself. The Navy had always been my job, my employer. While I knew what needed to be done to complete the mission, I always kept a piece of me back. A piece that I could pull out when I needed to be normal. Because let's face it, at the end of the day, my job is to kill people." When she tried to pull away, he held on just a little bit tighter. "No, let me finish. I'm not trying to scare you, but I need to get this out. We've never talked about my job in detail, which was by design. But I need to tell this story so I can better explain what you mean to me. Okay?"

She squeezed her arms around his waist tighter and nodded her head.

Noah continued speaking. "I get my orders, pack my shit, and I go across the ocean, desert, or wherever the mission takes me. Sometimes I rescue people. Families. Children. People important to the US Government. Other times I'm sent to neutralize a threat. All in the name of Uncle Sam. Bad people or not, someone loved them once. Mothers, fathers, siblings, children, spouses. They were loved. Yet, when I come into their lives, that person ceases to exist. There was always a part of me that knew and understood that." He took a deep inhale, the scent of coconut from her hair relaxed him as he rubbed his hands along her curvy form. "When I met you six years ago, you gave me peace. You gave my soul a place to rest when I was home. With you, I didn't think about the mission or the lives I'd taken. None of that mattered because you took care of me so damn good." He heard her laugh as her body shook.

"You took care of me, too," she whispered against his chest.

"Yeah, I did. But the call came, as it always does, and I had to leave. But something was different that time, and it scared me. No longer was I focused on the mission. My dreams were filled with your smile and the way your nose crinkles when you laugh. All I heard was the whisper of your voice as I slid my dick inside you. The only thing I felt was the softness of your skin as our naked bodies lay in bed. Every smell was laced with the aroma of your scent. Hell, I could even taste your essence on my tongue. I forgot to be a Navy SEAL and could only focus on being your man." He took a deep breath before he continued. "The memory of you became so much of a distraction that I took my eyes off the ball. I was wounded. Shot."

Her head whipped back, her eyes wide with worry. "What? When? Where?" Her hands began lifting his shirt to feel his bare skin.

"No. No. No. That's not the point of this story."

"But you were shot, Noah," she whispered. Fear evident in her tone.

Looking down at her, he kissed her soft lips. "Which is why I walked away. My head was all fucked up. I thought if I left you, my need for you would dissipate. My mind had it all twisted. I believed thinking of you was a bad thing, that I'd lost my edge because I'd been so caught up in you. When I stopped returning your emails and cut off contact, I buried myself in the job. I accepted every mission I could. Some without my unit, which Ethan and Daniel were part of. I was reckless as fuck and the family began to worry about me. Until about a year ago, when I realized I'd lost all emotion when doing my job. That piece of me, my humanity, that I kept sealed away and protected so I could come home and be a normal person with my parents, with the guys, and Adele? It was gone. Somewhere along the way, I'd lost who I was. Killing the enemy was like putting gas in my truck. Necessary. Required."

That was the hardest part of this confession. What if the man he truly was would never be good enough to measure up to the man she thought he was when they'd first met?

CHAPTER 23
Noah

Janae's sniffles reached his ears before her whispered words, "I'm sorry, Noah."

"No need to be sorry. You didn't cause it, Baby. It was me who did this. It was my own skewed thoughts about what you meant to me that got me in that position. I buried my feelings for you, and it took away so much more. When I got the call from Heath about Nicole, my focus was on making you pay. Hurting you for keeping my daughter away from me. Then I saw you. I saw her. All the screwed-up shit floating around in my head disappeared. The only thought in my head was how beautiful you still were. How much I'd missed you, kissing you, making love to you. When I saw Nicole's face and how much she looked like me, I could only thank God that I'd found such an amazing mother to have my child."

"Hmph. I didn't see any of that. You were kinda upset when you showed up at my door."

Shifting his hold on her, he rested his hands on her plump ass. "I was more upset that I'd cut off contact with you while you were pregnant with my child. My parents didn't raise me to be that type of man. I was filled with shame about what I'd done to you, to Nicole, and even to myself."

"You've made up for it with Nicole. She knows how much you love her. You're her hero, and nothing can change how she feels about you."

"But have I made it up to you? You still doubt how I feel about *you*. I'm not sure you believe me when I say my life isn't complete without you. So, this is what I want from you. Tell me what I need to do to convince you that you're the only woman for me."

"Tell me why you and the guys were fighting."

Noah knew that question was coming. That's what had prompted this conversation in the first place. "They didn't understand why they were just meeting you and Nicole today. They were hurt. Ethan, the tall blond married to Vanessa, has known me the longest. He thought I would have told him first. It wasn't that he's upset about you being here. Hell, he'd be the first one in line to protect you if I'm not around. He's already claimed his role as first uncle to Nicole."

Janae gave him a side glance. "What does that mean?"

"All good stuff. It's like a godfather, but since all the guys serve in that capacity, we have an order to things. Ethan's relegated Stefano to sixth uncle, the last in line," he laughed.

"Adele is going to get enough of you guys fucking with Stefano. Why don't you ever give him a break, Noah?"

"Awww, hell. We like the guy." At her look of disbelief, he smiled wide. "I promise. He's one of us, and if Adele has anything to do with it, he'll always be part of this family. If he hurts her or leaves or cheats on our sister, then that's another story. But since he's a smart man, that'll never happen. Don't feel bad for him, Janae. That fucker gives as good as he gets, then he smiles at all the women and pulls out that damn Italian accent to get them on his side. Just wait, you'll see soon enough. Trust me, that's the kind of shit he gets from Ethan on a regular basis. It's all fun and games. Those two would kill to protect each other."

"I thought it was because of me."

"I know."

"I was wrong."

Tilting his head, he kissed her deeply. "You were." Looking to the door, he whispered softly, even though he knew no one outside could hear them. "Janae, you can't leave me. I need you too much. You and Nicole are a part of me now. I lost a piece of myself when I left you the first time. I'm not willing to let you go again."

Just as she went to speak, the door handle jiggled, and a loud knock sounded on the door. Tyler's muffled voice could be heard. "Quit doing grown-up stuff and come out!"

Laughing, Noah looked at Janae. "Ready for round two?"

Mouth open in shock, she pointed at the door. "Did he just say...?"

"Yup. That's Tyler. If I didn't like him so much, I would tape his mouth shut." Grabbing her hand, he stood in front of her. "I love you, Janae Hayward. Maybe when I make you my wife you'll believe me."

"Wha—?"

"I'm gonna tell Stefano you two are in his office doing nasty stuff and making another baby!" Tyler laughed.

"Damnit, I thought Adele said this room was sound-proof. Fuck that, I'm taping his damn mouth shut," Noah growled before walking them to the door. Disengaging the lock, he flung it open, ready to take Tyler's head off. What he found instead was the entire group standing outside. Well, Stefano was off to the side and Monica had another full plate of food in her hands. Ethan stepped forward, his cheeks red with embarrassment. Vanessa stood next to him, arms crossed, eyes glaring at her husband with the promise of retribution. Uh oh. She must have heard about Ethan's reaction in the backyard.

"I'm sorry." Stepping closer, he wrapped Janae in his arms, giving her a huge bear hug. "Welcome to the family, sis." Pulling back, he looked at Noah before giving him a cheeky grin. "Did Noah tell you I'm first uncle?"

"What the fuck, Ethan? You can't just declare yourself first uncle," Tony yelled out.

"Yes, I can. I called dibs on the ballerina, so she's mine. Isn't that right baby?" Ethan looked over at Vanessa.

"Oh, no. That's between y'all. Come on, ladies," she said to the women. "Let's go, wobble-wobble. We need to get your ankles elevated. You're beginning to look like an oompa-loompa."

Pushing through the crowd of men, Monica approached Tyler. "Baby, does your big head baby with the ginormous appetite make me look fat?"

Noah wanted to laugh but knew it would probably make Monica cry. Daniel and Stefano had sudden coughing fits. Tony and Ethan looked at the paintings on the wall as if they were the most interesting thing in the world. Noah just stared at Tyler. He wanted to see how he talked his way out of this one. Because, yes, if he didn't know better, he'd think Monica was having twins.

"Honey, nothing could make you look fat. Our baby is strong and healthy. He just wants to make sure you're eating enough to keep the both of you that way. But, because you're carrying the future of our family, I agree with Vanessa. You should relax and rest. Don't worry about anything,

Sweetheart. You sit on the couch and be the queen you are."

Smooth move, man. Noah smiled as he gave a head nod to Tyler.

"Okay, thanks Ty," Monica replied before turning to the women and sticking her tongue out. Noah almost laughed at the childish gesture.

She turned and began making her way down the hallway to the family room before pausing to look at Tyler. "Um, can you bring me some ice cream when you finish?"

"Ano—Um, yes, absolutely. What kind?"

Her eyes cut back at him, as if trying to figure out what he hadn't said. "The pralines and cream one."

"You got it, baby," Tyler replied with a smile.

After she'd walked away and was out of sight, the guys all walked into Stefano's office, closed the door, and burst out laughing.

"Man, you were quick on your feet," Daniel praised with a two-finger salute.

"Monica will probably make Vanessa feel guilty for calling her that crazy name," Tony responded with a smirk.

"Adele calls her that, too. I think it's because Monica's usually so hyper-focused on her weight and fitness due to the military. With that big head baby growing in her stomach she can't," Ethan stated as if he was an expert on the matter.

Tyler threw a pen at him. "Don't call my baby Big Head, dude. My baby's going to be perfect."

"Yeah, he'll have a perfectly Big Head," Stefano teased with a smile.

All the guys started laughing and pointing at Tyler. When Stefano joined in on the joke, you knew you were done. That guy was too damn serious if you asked Noah. Stefano grabbed a bottle of scotch from a hidden shelf and poured everyone a drink. The house had enough rooms for all of them to stay over, and the living room could be converted to a kids' zone, so no one was worried about drinking.

Ethan came to stand next to Noah. "When are you going to marry her?"

The question had been floating around Noah's mind for a while now. There was no question about *IF* he would marry her. There was only a question about the timing. "As soon as we can arrange it. I want my parents in town and hers as well. When we do this, I want it done the right way."

"Do your parents know?" Tyler asked, joining the two men.

"They do."

Ethan sighed. "Oh, boy. What did your dad have to say?"

"Hell, I want to know how Mama Braddock responded. To be so small, your momma is a firecracker," Tyler laughed.

"Neither of them was happy with me, but once I sent them a picture of Janae and Nicole, they got over it. Now all my mom can talk about is her amazingly talented granddaughter and when she can see them in person. I think they'll be making a trip over this way sooner than we expect."

Noah's attention was pulled away by the laughter of Daniel, Stefano, and Tony. He thought about the life ahead of him and smiled at the picture playing in his mind. Weekend get-togethers with family and friends, laughter all around him, kids running around and playing, and their wives or significant others bonding as sisters should. He nodded to himself as he came to a decision about his future. He'd waited long enough. It was time he started down a new path. His retirement papers would be submitted next week.

*****

A few days later, Noah and Janae sat on the couch watching a movie. Nicole was down for an afternoon nap after returning from a playdate over at Ethan and Vanessa's house. Grabbing her hand in his, he looked down at the woman lying in his arms. "Marry me, Janae."

Lifting her head, she had a look of shock on her face. "What?"

"Marry me. I know you may think it's too soon, but I know the time is right." As she sat up, looking at him in silence, his neck began to warm with heat and embarrassment.

"Wh-Wh-What about my parents? Your parents? Wait? When do you want to get married?" She was rambling, but he didn't care.

"Baby, you had to know this day was coming. I want to marry you. Nicole should have my last name. You should have my ring on your finger. We can arrange it whenever you want. I want both sets of parents there, and Heath, Stephanie, and the girls have to get here as well." He watched as tears glistened in her eyes. "And as for a ring," he reached behind him to the console table positioned next to the couch and picked up the box he'd placed there earlier. Sliding off the couch, he knelt in front of her and opened the box. "Marry me, Janae. You've given me the piece of my soul I'd thought was lost to me forever. I love you. I will be your protector, your lover, and the father of any and all children you choose to grace me with for as long as I live. Marry me."

"Yes," she yelled, jumping into his arms. "Yes, I'll marry you. You amazing, wonderful man! Oh, I have to call Adele and Vanessa and Monica."

"You can call them in a minute. First, I want my engagement gift. I just have to unwrap it." Just as he began to peel her t-shirt from her body, his phone rang, and his blood turned cold. He had a special ring for his command. Whenever he got a call with the special tone, he knew exactly what it was for, so it could never be missed. But today was not the day he wanted this call to come through. He needed more time. They were too new. Things were too tenuous right now.

Looking down at her, he hoped his eyes didn't betray the feelings swirling inside him.

"What's wrong?"

"I have to answer, Babe. It's my command." Standing, he went over to the table and grabbed up the phone, knowing this would be the greatest test of their relationship. He just hoped they could survive.

CHAPTER 24
Janae

One month later...

Janae was a bundle of nerves. Nicole was feeling her stress and acting out. It had gotten so bad, the ladies had begun rotating nights when Nicole would stay at their house. Adele took the most nights since she and Stefano had a full staff to help with the kids. Janae felt horrible about depending on them so much, but she was quickly finding out this was just how this family took care of each other. Tonight, since it was a Friday, Vanessa and Ethan had taken her, promising to give her a weekend of fun while Janae relaxed.

After the call came in that fateful day, Noah had been gone within twenty-four hours. Just enough time to call his parents, inform the rest of their group, and spend some final hours with her and Nicole. Even though she was better prepared this time, she was still a nervous wreck. She'd been tempted to beg, plead, and bargain for Noah not to leave. But she didn't let the words exit her mouth. This was the hard part of life when you loved a military man. Sometimes they had to leave at the drop of a hat, without notice, and without warning.

She'd gotten a crash-course in what that meant for her and Noah. Within hours of his departure, she had a steady rotation of people at her door. Adele would pick up Nicole for a playdate. Monica would come to spend time with Janae, elevating her feet and telling crazy stories about her time in the Marines. Ethan and Vanessa came over to cookout—since, according to Ethan, he was a master chef—which somehow turned into a family event when Tyler called to check on her and Ethan picked up the phone. Monica's father, who had a running competition with Ethan about who grilled the best, showed up with two slabs of ribs. Already seasoned and tenderized for some reason. Of course, Monica's sister, Charity, came along as well, which was interesting since she'd never seen Charity and Daniel in the same space. The heat between those two almost set the house on fire. She still laughed at the conversation she had with Monica.

"So, um, your sister and Daniel?"

Rolling her eyes, Monica ate another spoonful of potato salad. "Don't make me throw up my food."

"Oh, Gawd, not that!" Janae teased. "You want something to drink?" At Monica's nod, Janae grabbed another bottle of water and handed it to the pregnant woman.

Monica glanced at her sister and Daniel trying to play coy with each other. Shaking her head, she sighed. "I've tried to tell her that man plays for keeps. She keeps saying how she has it under control, but I don't think she does."

Janae looked over her shoulder at the two. "From what I can tell, she seems to have his nose wide open. That man is not letting up. At least she's smiling. Is she interested in him the same way?"

Taking a few more bites of her food, Monica looked across the room at the couple and nodded. "I think she is. My sister and I are of the same ilk. We saw how our mother's death impacted our father, and we both swore to never love someone that much." She turned her face to Janae and smiled. "That didn't work out so well for me since I love Tyler's crazy ass as if he were meant for me."

Janae's heart twisted. She felt the same way about Noah. What if something happened to him while he was over there? Now that she better understood the situation, she was filled with fear and worry that this time, he wouldn't come home. Getting her mind back on the conversation, she smirked at Monica. "You two *are* made for each other. He's crazy and you're mean. It's a perfect match," Janae teased before jumping out of the way.

"Woman, get over here so I can pinch you. You can't call me mean, Janae. Adele!" Monica called out to the other woman for help.

Janae laughed at the disgruntled look on Monica's face since they both knew there was no way she could lift from the couch in her current situation.

Janae danced out of her reach, "If you can get up and catch me, I'll let you pinch me." Knowing the woman couldn't move faster than a snail at this point, Janae felt safe. Until Vanessa came up and pinched her on the butt. "Ow!"

Laughing at Janae's pouting face, Vanessa made her way outside to Ethan. "That's what you get. Don't tease our oompa-loompa. We love her, even if she is mean."

The ding of the microwave brought her back to the present. Her leftover dinner from earlier tonight was ready. Thinking of the women, she couldn't help but laugh at their antics. These people made life a little bit easier for her to deal with. Looking back, she felt ashamed of her thoughts when Noah initially wanted her to meet his friends in Virginia. The fear of being rejected was a real thing, but she knew most of it stemmed from her experiences back home.

Virginia was now her home and she was glad she'd made the move. After two weeks of Noah being away, he'd called to check-in. During their conversation, he'd demanded she make the final move to Virginia. Told her when he came home, he wanted to know his family was waiting for him. No matter how many arguments she had, he always countered with something else. The man had an answer for everything. Of course, she had to give a cursory protest, but she wanted to be waiting for him at their home just as much he wanted her there. Stefano, magic man that he was, had her home in Jacksonville packed and moved within five days. Her house was on the market, and she'd given notice to her employer that she was relocating.

Everything happened so fast, her head was spinning. Her parents were upset at first and wanted her to slow down, to think about what she was doing. She thought they were more concerned with not seeing Nicole each week more than anything. Funny how strict, tough parents became mushy, gushy softies when it came to their grandchildren. According to her dad, they planned to take a trip to Virginia next week *'to see what all the fuss is about.'*

Standing, she looked at the clock and noted it was just after seven in the evening. She wanted to call Vanessa and check on Nicole, but refrained. Nicole was well cared for, and Janae never had to worry. Noah had been right when he'd described the people he claimed as his family. They took care of each other. Their kids were all taken care of by the others. The men protected and cared for their women. No matter where in the world Noah was called, Janae knew she and Nicole would be in good hands. Her finger twisted the engagement ring sitting on her ring finger. That motion made her feel closer to Noah and wetness pooled in her eyes as she prayed for his safe return. She just wanted her man home, in her arms, or playing with their daughter, or cutting up in the backyard with his brothers.

She wanted Noah home.

Just as she moved to grab another glass of wine, she heard a sound at the front door. No one should be entering their home. Thinking quickly, she slid across the kitchen floor to the hidden space under the cabinet. Pressing her fingerprint against the readers, she heard the small door click open and reached inside. Janae grabbed the .45 she'd been trained to use in the past few months. Keeping the gun safety on, she knew Ethan and Tyler had trained her well. She could remove the safety and fire within a millisecond. As she waited for bated breath, she heard a thump on the floor, as if something dropped. Then heavy footsteps moving in the direction of the kitchen.

"Who the fuck—"

"Janae, sweetheart—"

They spoke at the same time, and Janae let a small scream escape. "Noah," she cried, placing the weapon down and running into his arms. "You're home! You're home," she repeated while kissing him on every inch of skin she could see.

"Baby, I'm home. I missed you so fucking much."

She felt his embrace tighten. Her heart constricted with joy. Noah was safe, alive, and home. "I was so worried about you. I'm so glad you're home."

"Where's our baby girl?"

"At her auntie Vanessa's for the weekend. Wait a minute! Did they know you were coming home?" Legs wrapped around his waist, arms on his shoulders, and her hands cradling his face, she gave her man a stern look. "Did you plan this?"

Noah began walking them up the stairs to the master bedroom. "I'm not telling. All I know is, I'm home where I belong, my woman is happy to see me, and my daughter is being spoiled by her aunt and uncle. Did you hear that?"

Jumping, she twisted her head in different directions. "No. What is it?"

"Exactly. Nothing but silence. It's time for you to give me a homecoming present." Noah leaned over and placed her on the bed in front of him. "You are so goddamned beautiful."

"You're not so bad yourself," she smiled, reaching up to rub her hand down his face. Noah brought his lips to hers, giving her a kiss meant to curl her toes, and he did.

If getting naked were an Olympic sport, Janae would have won the gold. She wanted Noah inside her. Needed to feel him against her bare skin. Breaking their kiss, she ran her fingers down his chiseled jaw. "I need you."

Positioning himself above her, Noah rested his hips between her soft thighs as his cock nestled against her slick skin. "You have me."

He began kissing her neck and nibbling at her breasts, while his hand traveled down her body back to her pulsing, throbbing center. Using his fingers, he entered her slick pussy, the thickness of his digits bringing a moan to her lips. Noah smiled down at her as she spread her legs wider for him, reveling in the intensity of the feelings coursing through her body.

His low moans reached her ears as she squirmed underneath him. Her breath released in rapid pants as he teased and tantalized her highly sensitized body. Janae knew she was going to die from the pleasure and she didn't care one bit. Noah pressed a spot inside her channel, and she released raw scream as her body was flung into a body-quivering orgasm.

"That's it, sweetheart. Damn, I've missed you so much. I want all of you, and I don't want you to hold anything back," he growled in her ear, as she came down from her powerful orgasm.

Janae couldn't think straight. Her mind could only conjure up the idea of making love to Noah.

Noah moved his body into position, aligning the head of his cock with her slick opening. She gave him a sultry smile before grabbing at the short strands of his hair, pulling his face down to her as she spread her legs a bit wider. His body sank down onto hers. She sighed into his mouth as she felt the mushroomed head of his cock begin to breach her body. Feeling Noah's steel length slide into her, she looked into his eyes and saw his need, desire, and love reflected. Even though she was soaking wet, he still had to enter her slowly due to his size. Being with him like this felt like her very own Heaven on Earth.

Pushing his thick cock in and out of her body, slowly sliding inside inch by inch, he managed to embed himself to the hilt. She couldn't stifle the loud moan that escaped her lips. Noah's breathing was harsh, deep, the sound battering her ears as he leaned his head down next to her. "Give me a minute. If I don't slow down, this won't end the way I want."

Janae finally found her voice. "It feels good to me no matter what," she moaned, kissing his chiseled jaw.

"It's about to feel a whole lot better." Noah began to glide in and out, the pull of his thick member rubbing against her walls. She felt so full; the length of him was almost too much to handle. It was so intense, tears leaked from her eyes. As their bodies writhed together, neither of them could speak a coherent word. The only sounds in the room were grunts and groans as they rode out the powerful emotions they created in each other. Wrapping her arms around his neck as he plunged in and out of her body, she lifted her legs and placed them around his waist as Noah continued to take her to the peak of pleasure.

"Come for me, Janae. Give it to me," Noah demanded.

Unable to hold back any longer, she felt her body clench as the sensation roared through her like a freight train. Her mouth opened in a silent scream as she clenched around his thick member. As she was in the throes of her orgasm, he positioned his arms around her body and fucked her like there was no tomorrow. Just as his body stilled and she felt his cock begin to pulse inside of her, she heard his whispered words.

"I love you so fucking much. I'm finally home."

Gripping him tighter, there was so much she wanted to say but the words wouldn't come out. She tried to convey how she was feeling in the strength of her embrace and the softness of her kisses.

After a few moments, Noah shifted to the side, bringing her body flush with his. "Can we schedule the wedding for thirty-days from now?"

Laughing at him, because clearly, he was overcome by how good it felt to back in her arms, she shook her head. "Not enough time. What about six months?"

Shifting them, he placed her body on top of his. Her legs spread wide as she rested her core over his quickly rising cock. "Three months, Noah. I need time to get everything situated. We need dresses and tuxedos for the wedding party. I'll need all the ladies to help and Monica is about to give birth soon, plus we have the Special Olympics event next weekend. I need time."

Noah lifted her body just enough to allow the thick steel between his legs to penetrate her body. "Unless you want to be pregnant when you walk down the aisle, you'll move the date up. I'm home. My retirement papers have been turned in. My job with the guys at Overwatch is waiting for me. Only thing I need now is to see you walk down the aisle and become my wife."

He began lifting his hips, stroking her inside with the miracle appendage she loved so much. "But... But..."

"Give me what I want, baby." Grabbing her hips, he pulled her down against him hard before increasing his pace. "Tell me what I want to hear, Janae."

Her mind blanked. She looked down at Noah and nodded. "Yes, whatever you want. Whenever you want."

"That's what I thought. Don't worry, I'll take care of everything."

Janae could only focus on the sensation of pleasure coursing through her limbs. Noah was home, and she couldn't be happier.

EPILOGUE

"Owen Braddock! If you don't get your little behind over here right now." Janae ran around the backyard like a chicken with her head cut off. Her one-year-old son, who took after not only his father but every single one of his uncles, decided today was the day he wanted to become a nudist.

"Daddy, why is baby Owen running around without his clothes on?" Sophia asked Stefano as he walked her over to the table to grab some food.

"Because he's a very independent little boy who likes to give his momma fits," he said, laughing at the scene in front of him.

"Like I give to momma?"

All the guys around him laughed. "Yes, baby. Just like that. But you know, little Michael is just like your cousin Owen. Those two are going to get into a lot of trouble when they get older."

Noah stepped outside at that very moment. "Nope, my son's going to be an angel." Just then, Janae called out to him.

"Noah! If you don't grab your son and get him to put some clothes on, I'm running away."

Loud laughter followed him as he moved left to intercept the little boy running circles around his mother. How could such a tiny person move so fast? "Oh, no you don't." Grabbing up his son, he began marching back to the house. "Listen, young man, you're not getting daddy in trouble today. You're gonna get some swimmers and shorts on before you go into the pool. Got it?"

His son gave him a shrewd look, his hazel-green eyes stared back at him with intelligence that shouldn't be present in a child so young. "Hi, Daddy! Mommy run and chase!" Owen bent over in a deep belly laugh as if having his mother scramble after a naked, squirming child was the funniest thing ever.

"Kid, I can see you're gonna give your mommy and me a run for our money." Noah moved quickly to get his son dressed and back outside with his cousins.

Once he was back outside, Nicole got him into the kiddie pool with the other kids around his age. Nicole and Damian, Ethan and Vanessa's son, were the big kids of the bunch, so they made sure to lord their power over the younger children. He wasn't bothered though, he knew they'd keep a watchful eye on the smaller kids. And if there was something they couldn't handle, one of the adults would step in.

Taking a swig of soda, he couldn't help but be happy with where his life was. Today was a good day for him and his brothers. Business at Overwatch Security was damn good. Their families were flourishing, and his brothers were happy. Well, most of them anyway, he thought before glancing over at Daniel and Charity who were off-again, and then to Tony who was ignoring everyone. The woman he thought Tony was in love with had married another man. He knew those two would figure it out soon enough.

"Hey, Baby. Thank you for wrangling the kid." Janae walked up to him and gave him a soft kiss.

"Not a problem. I'm your hero, right? That means wrestling our kids to behave when needed." Pulling her closer to his side, he gave thanks for whatever he'd done in his life to bring Janae into his world.

"Heath and Stephanie will be here in an hour. They got in late last night and needed a bit more rest."

"Okay, that's fine." It would be good to see his friends and their family. It had been more than six months since he'd last seen him. At that time, Heath had been talking retirement. Noah hoped he was serious because he had a proposition for him. All the guys were on board with bringing Heath onto the team if he wanted it. He wouldn't be an equal partner, but he also wouldn't have to start at the bottom.

"Oh, I heard from my mom. They're having a blast on the cruise with your mom and dad. I think those four are getting into more trouble than we thought. Whose idea was it to see if they'd all get along?"

Noah smiled. Shortly after the wedding, the two older couples seemed to strike up a close friendship. They'd been to Las Vegas, Niagara Falls, and to professional football games in multiple states. Now they were on a seven-day cruise to the Caribbean. Maybe being retired wasn't such a bad thing after all. "Not mine. I know my parents are incorrigible. I think they all gravitated to each other like moths to a flame."

Wrapping her arms around his waist, she rested her head on his chest. "If you say so, big guy." They both heard the doorbell ring. "I'll get it."

"Nah, it's okay. I got it. You rest, sweetheart."

Noah walked to the door, thinking it was Heath and Stephanie. It wasn't. Cole Reynolds, or Hawk as they called him, stood at the door. Hawk worked with them at Overwatch and was one of the best guys they'd brought in. While all the guys they worked with were welcome to stop by at any time, Cole seemed to be more of a loner. He focused on work, he went home, and he didn't socialize much, no matter how many times the offer was extended. Former Army Delta, Hawk was one of their deadliest assets. "Hey, Hawk. What's up, man? Come in. Want a beer?" He offered, motioning towards the kitchen.

"Hey, Ghost. Nah, I'm good. You know that issue I was helping my lady with?"

It took Noah a moment to remember. He'd been out of town at his in-laws' house with shit started to go down with Hawk's lady cop. "Yeah, the guys told me about it. That shit getting hot again?"

"Yeah, I think I got a lead. I know you guys are having a family weekend, but I need to update everyone on the latest. We can't waste time next week." Hawk stood at the foyer, but Noah didn't want him to feel out of place.

"Come on inside. If I don't offer you something to eat, Janae will tear me a new one. All the guys are out back." Stepping into the backyard, Noah saw eyes turn to Hawk as he strolled across the yard to greet some of the team.

"Cole? Are you hungry?" Janae was walking over to the man with a cold beer.

"I could eat," he answered with a smile.

"I just bet. Come on, grab something first, then you guys can talk business."

A bevy of male voices yelled out, "What? We're not working! Come on, Janae, we didn't do anything."

Once they were out of earshot, Noah moved to the group of men. "It's all good fellas. I think Hawk is looking for some help to close a tricky situation with his lady. I think it may be time to go hunting."

~ FIN ~

Thank You!

Thank you for supporting my writing. It truly means a lot to me. If you enjoyed **Homecoming**, Noah and Janae's story, please take a few moments to leave a review on the platform where this book was purchased.

As you may know, reviews help motivate authors as we continue writing and bringing you great stories. The more reviews on a book, the more visible it becomes to other readers.

Thank you for your support!

* * * * *

Keep swiping to read an excerpt from **Persuade Me.**

Persuade Me
Summary

~ **_Sometimes good and evil must coexist to bring about the reckoning._** ~

Ebony - _I've never begged for anything. Until the day I begged him to save my life._

Fear was not a word I used. Failure had never been an option. Even as life threw me curveballs on a regular basis, I powered through. My job as a police officer drove me to do better, be better than anyone else, and to protect those who needed my help. My position as President of the Fairfax Chapter of Lady Guardians instilled a sense of sisterhood and passion for my community. I'm proud of the person I've become and have no regrets about the life I've lived. Well, except one--and it happens to be the man hovering over my body as I bleed out on my front lawn.

Cole - _Life on the other side wasn't all it was cracked up to be, but my forgiveness will be found in the unlikeliest of places._

The day I came home to find my beautiful neighbor on the verge of death, my world shifted. She'd seen me when all I wanted to do was hide, not allowing me to wallow in my guilt and memories. The things I'd seen in combat, scarred me for life, changing me into someone I hardly recognized. But it didn't matter to her. Now someone had hurt her. The woman I desired from afar, even as I knew it was best that I stayed on my side of the street. I was no good for her. For anyone. But someone had tried to harm her, and that just wouldn't do at all.

CHAPTER 1

Ebony

Pain radiated through her body as she realized she'd been shot. Her face was wet from the steady flow of tears falling from her eyes. Ebony lay in the front yard of her home as her life seeped out into the grass. Eyes wide, but blurry from pain, she tried to focus on the sights and sounds around her. The sky above her was a gorgeous light blue, with small clouds floating by, breaking up the view. The only thing she heard around her was the whizzing of vehicles as they drove down the street.

A low keening noise sounded in the silence. It was like an animal in distress. Ebony's ears picked up the wail, but it seemed to be muffled, far away. As she tried to move her lips to call out, to yell for someone to call 9-1-1, she realized the sound was coming from her. Fear coursed through her mind, and wetness continued to fall from her eyes.

It couldn't end this way.

There was too much still left to do.

It wasn't her time to die.

She had people who loved her. People who wanted her to live. She'd be damned if her last breath would be taken like this. Lying in a pool of her own blood. Alone.

Digging her fingers into the dirt as she twisted in pain, she felt the fresh dirt under her nails. Wouldn't it be some bullshit if these were her last moments on earth? A seasoned police officer with more than a decade of service under her belt, it was almost embarrassing that she'd been caught off-guard.

When the sound of the weapon firing met her ears, she'd pulled her service-issued gun from its holster, ready to respond to the threat. No matter how fast she was, it had already been too late. Hot lead filled her body, the heat slicing through her soft flesh.

The shock came first. Then the pain.

Falling to the ground, she'd tried to fight the convoluted thoughts going through her mind. During her years of being a cop, she'd come across her fair share of criminals, thugs, and murderers. Hell, she'd even been shot before and lived to tell the tale. Those times she'd been actively engaged, ready to risk her life to bring down her target. Injury or death had been an expected outcome.

Today was not one of those situations. There was no preparation for this. Ebony hadn't been going after a criminal or harassing a potential suspect. No, this time, she'd been coming home after finishing up a long ass shift. She'd been working extra hours on a case dealing with human trafficking, and something about it was getting to her. Things weren't adding up. She was missing something, and that shit bothered her.

Bone tired and ready to crash for the next two days, she wasn't focused on her surroundings. Her mind was prepared to shut down, even if only for a few hours. She'd been thinking long and hard about a hot shower and a cold beer. Ebony had let her guard down for only a few moments, which she knew never to do.

Within seconds, her world was thrown off its axis.

Now she lay in the dirt and grass in front of her home—her safe space—with a bullet lodged inside her. Moving her head to the side, she noticed the blood pooling on top of her clothing, the dark red liquid seeping into the grass.

Wincing with pain as she shifted, Ebony "Diamond" Thompson, tried to think of a way out of this. She wasn't going out without a fight. The voice of Deuce, the Vice President of the Lady Guardians, entered her mind, and she almost smiled at the thought of her friend.

Deuce would pull out these sayings from her time in the Marine Corps that would throw everyone for a loop. They'd be sitting around the club, shooting the shit, and having a drink, doing nothing much. Then BAM! Deuce would pull out one of her favorite sayings. Ebony's favorite was: 'Blood makes the grass grow. Marines make the blood flow. Kill! Kill! Kill!'

Ebony could feel a small chuckle bubble through her as she thought about her longtime friend and partner in crime. Deuce would kick her ass if she died this way. Ebony tried to roll over, but a sharp sting clawed its way through her chest. Falling back down, she let out a deep breath.

Well, if she died on her lawn, her grass would be nice and green. At least according to Deuce and the US Marine Corps. Her Homeowner's Association would appreciate that. They were a bunch of prudes who had nothing else better to do but get in other people's business.

Deuce would probably kill everyone in her path when she found out what happened to Ebony. Even after knowing her for ten years, Ebony still held onto a healthy dose of fear for her best friend. Laughing a little at the thought of Deuce's small five-foot-six-inch frame going all Marine Corps revenge killer, she groaned as the pain intensified inside her body. Wincing, she fought to control the need to close her eyes and wait for the inevitable.

Fuck this shit. She needed to fight.

"Help me," she whispered. Her voice was low, and where she lay was shielded by the hedges on each side of her yard. It was mid-afternoon, so not many people in her lovely, middle-class neighborhood were at home. She didn't expect anyone to have heard the shot. Even if they did, they might not have realized what the sound was.

Feeling herself getting weaker by the minute, she tried to pull her cell phone from her pocket. "Help me," she prayed to whoever was listening.

Sobs tore from her body as she accepted what was happening. Someone wanted her dead. They'd learned where she lived. Waited until she was alone, with her guard down. The motherfucker shot her. And she had no idea who it could be.

Her list of enemies was too long to think about, and her mind was too garbled to think clearly. She'd put a lot of people behind bars over the years. Even had a few complaints filed against her for excessive force, but none of those charges stuck. It wasn't her fault some men were bitch ass pansies who couldn't take getting their ass kicked by a woman.

She wasn't worried about finding the perpetrator—not much anyway. Her brothers and sisters in blue would find out who did this to her. Hell, Deuce would probably find the shooter before they did.

If only she could tell her friend thank you for all the times she'd had her back. For all the ways she'd supported Ebony in her role as President of their Lady Guardians chapter.

Ebony's vision began to fade. Blackness converged on the edges of her eyes. She was going into shock from blood loss. She couldn't even feel the pain anymore. Maybe this wasn't so bad after all. Her life would slip away as if she were falling asleep.

For thirty-three years, she'd lived a life that others would envy. Had grown up with two amazing parents who'd loved and supported her without question. Achieved the career she'd dreamed of: catching the bad guys and making the streets better. And rode a badass motorcycle daily. Who wouldn't want a life like that?

Her only regret was that she was going to die alone. No husband. Not even an ex-husband. No boyfriend who'd miss her if she didn't call him to check-in and share their days. Children hadn't been in the plan for her, especially with her career choice. The dangers were too many. She didn't want to risk not coming home one night and leaving her child on their own, their only parent dead at the hands of a criminal.

If she'd had a long-time boyfriend or husband, maybe it would have been different. But she didn't. There was only her mother and her little sister. Her father had passed away from a massive heart attack six months after she'd graduated from the Police Academy.

For months he kept repeating how proud he was of her. He'd brag to all his friends that his daughter, his princess, was at the top of her graduating class. Six months after she'd walked across that platform, he'd gone to work one day, and never made it back home.

Her breath was shallow as she felt her heartbeat slowing down. The only good thing about this situation was that she'd get to see her father again. They could look down on her mother and sister and make sure they were doing okay. Protect them from up high, just as she and her father protected them while on this earth.

With one last surge of energy, she pulled her cell phone from her pocket. The small device in her hands, she managed to press the nine- and the one- before it fell from her fingers.

"I'm sorry, momma," she tried to say, but the words came out mumbled.

"Hey!"

A loud voice called out to her, but she had no energy to respond. Relief flooded her body when she heard someone running in her direction.

"Ebony! Can you hear me? Fuck!" She heard fumbling before he spoke again. "Yeah, we need an ambulance. My neighbor's been shot. She's a police officer. I don't know how long she's been out here. I just got home." He paused. "Okay, let me check. Hold on."

She felt his hands on her body. She was about to die, and all she could think about was how good his touch felt. As soon as he'd spoken above her, she'd recognized his voice. The fine ass guy across the street. *Cole.* The one whose look was so intense, she felt butterflies in her stomach every time they crossed paths.

There was something about him that pulled her closer, made her want to know him better. But she hadn't been willing to put herself out there, so she refrained from approaching him. There were so many reasons not to go down that path. Hot naked sex was all well and good, but it would be rude to kick the guy out of her bed once she had her fill, only to see him every morning when she left for work.

Plus, there was also the possibility that even if she approached him, it wouldn't turn out the way she wanted. What if he rejected her? What if she wasn't his type?

Maybe he already had a woman who made his toes curl and fucked him until he was weak in the knees. Even with all those negative thoughts, it didn't mean he didn't fill her dreams at night. Because he sure as fuck did. And when she woke up, her pussy would be wet and the gasp still on her lips from the phantom dick that had been giving it to her for hours as she slept.

It didn't matter if she'd pictured his large, pale body between her dark legs. Or his rough beard scratching against the soft skin of her inner thighs as his mouth devoured her pussy. Not to mention her silent wish that he had a thick, fat dick to slide inside her body, every thrust making her moan with need and desire.

No. None of that mattered. Why? Because she'd been too chicken-shit to say anything to him.

Lying here with her life fading away, she wished she'd gone after what she wanted. Who cares if she crashed and burned? At least she would have tried. With the way he eyeballed her whenever she stepped outside of her house, she didn't think he would've pushed her away.

"Can you talk? Ebony! Sweetheart, open your eyes for me." His rough voice called out to her. The tone strained with something akin to fear.

She tried to respond. Oh, how she tried to say something—*do* something—but her throat was clogged from her tears and lids were too heavy to lift. Ebony fought against the darkness threatening to take her away. Consolidating all her strength into the one movement, she focused her gaze on the man hovering above her.

"Hey, Beautiful. There you are. Keep those gorgeous browns open for me. Can you do that? An ambulance is on the way, but I need you to stay with me. Okay?" Taking off his shirt, he rolled it up and placed it under her head. "Who did this to you?" At her silence, he continued. "Ebony, talk to me. Is this related to your job?"

Licking her lips, she managed to squeak out a response. "Don't... know."

"It's okay. I'm here. I can hear the sirens now." Her eyes began to close again, but his hand cradled her face. "Stay with me. Open those eyes for me, sweetheart. Just a little bit longer." Looking up from her, he began speaking to others who'd started crowding around.

"Yes, the ambulance was called. They'll be here soon. No, I don't know what happened. Just move back a little."

Of course, while she lay here hoping someone would come to help her, not a person was in sight. Now that her hunky, drop-dead sexy neighbor had shown up, everyone had come out of the woodworks. *Figures.*

Turning his green gaze back to her, he stared at her face as if memorizing her features. Ebony marveled at just how good looking he was. Dark hair covered his head and face, giving him a rough edge. She could tell, even beneath it all, that his chin was firm, strong. His lips were perfectly shaped, with just enough thickness to make kissing him an absolute pleasure.

His upper body was broad, his chest and arms sculpted with muscles on top of muscles. Cole was much taller than her as well, at least six feet four inches. For her, standing five feet ten inches in socks, he was the perfect height. She'd pictured herself climbing him like a spider-monkey a few times. If only she'd had the chance to get a taste of him before meeting her maker. Shit was just unfair.

Smiling down at her, he spoke again, "They're pulling up now. Keep those eyes on me a little longer."

Ebony struggled a bit. Being strong was all well and good, but she didn't want to be in that ambulance alone. Not today. Today, she needed someone by her side. Cole had just been selected for the job.

As if reading her mind, he rubbed a hand down her arm. "I'm not going anywhere. I'm here. Hell," he gave a low laugh, "I'd wanted to know you better but not like this." Glancing over his shoulder, he waved his hand in the air. "All right, sweetheart, I need to let the paramedics take care of you. Don't worry. I'm only stepping back for a minute."

Cole moved away to allow the professionals to step closer. She wanted to hold his hand, pull him back to her. Ebony didn't want to let him go. It was the first time in her life she needed someone to be there for her.

"Cole," she managed to whisper. "Please. Don't go."

* * * * *

Persuade Me is Available for purchase in both ebook and print.

About the Author

Reana Malori is a USA Today Bestselling Author of Contemporary romance focusing on Multicultural / Interracial couples. She firmly believes that love in all its forms should be celebrated and her stories reflect that belief. She hopes to weave stories that pull the reader into her world and helps them to share in her universe, even if only for a short time.

An avid reader since the age of fourteen, she decided to pursue her passion in 2009 and released her first novella, To Love a Marine. Since then, she has released more than 30 books of varying lengths, to include Weekend Fling, Escape to Heaven, Finding Faith, Conall and Flawless.

When not writing, you can most often find her enjoying a good book as she is, first and foremost, a romance reader. Reana currently resides in Montclair, Virginia with her husband and two sons who keep her busy laughing, having fun, and making sure she doesn't take herself too seriously.

Also by Reana Malori
Available at Your Favorite Online Retailer
****

Claiming Lana
Closer to You
Conall (Irish Sugar)
Falling Into Love (w/ Janet Eckford)
Finding Faith
Flawless (F'd Up Fairy Tales)
Losing Control
Promise Me
Queen of Spades (The Player's Club)
Raven's Crown (The Royal Court)
Salvation: The Italian's Story
Secret Devotion
Spellbound
Stay (Naughty Nanny)
Stay With Me
Tangled Lies
The Long Shot
Three Wishes
To Love a Marine
Unwrapping a Marriage (w/ Michel Prince)
What Matters Most
Workout Partners

Angel Hearts
Dark Angel (Book 1)
Broken Angel (Book 2)

Heaven on Earth
Escape to Heaven
Redemption
Sacrifice
Homecoming

Made in the USA
Middletown, DE
15 October 2023

40803654R00210